Copyright © 2020 by A.J. Rivers

All rights reserved.

No part of this book may be reproduced in any form or by any electronic or mechanical means, including information storage and retrieval systems, without written permission from the author, except for the use of brief quotations in a book review.

❦ Created with Vellum

THE GIRL IN DANGEROUS WATERS

A.J. RIVERS

PROLOGUE

ONE YEAR AGO...

"A single bullet wound to the base of the skull."

"Sounds like an execution. Were there any other injuries?" I ask.

"Nothing separate from what he was already recovering from in the hospital," the medical examiner tells me. "The abrasions on his face are from the sand."

I nod.

"Thank you," I tell her.

Tightly coiled dark hair bound up in a ponytail at the back of her head bounces slightly as she pulls the sheet back up over Greg's face. The sight of it catches my breath in my throat. I've seen it before, but this time there's no question. I know it's him.

I take a step back, waiting for her to slide the slab back into the morgue drawer and close the heavy metal door over it. Our eyes meet. She gives me a look that's something close to pity. It's a look I've been getting a lot recently, but I've more than had my fill. Without another word, I turn and leave.

Stepping out into the hallway is a relief. The last time I was in a morgue was in the hospital. I was stretched out on one of those slabs, drugged, and hidden behind the heavy metal door. Dean rescued me from the drawer before I froze to death, but there is no rescuing Greg. No getting him out. He will lie there alone in the dark and cold while we try to unravel what happened to him.

"He wasn't supposed to leave alone," I say, storming down the hallway past Eric, who waits for me against the wall. "He was supposed to wait at the hospital until he could be discharged with a guard. What was he thinking, walking out of that hospital without one of us? Or at least another agent?"

"Did Dr. Galvan find out anything else?" he asks.

"Same as the initial findings. Single bullet hole to the back of the head. She said there were no other signs of injury. I guess you don't really need any other injuries when you get a point-blank hole to the skull," I explain.

He follows me through the building and out into the thin, bright sunlight of the afternoon. The towering mirrored building is stark and sterile. The trees planted along the sidewalk in front of it don't do much to soften its appearance. Somehow the rays of light bouncing off the sharp corners and expanses of metal and glass make them feel colder.

"Sounds like an execution," Eric muses.

"That's exactly what I said," I tell him, yanking gloves onto my hands. But there's something about it that doesn't sit well with me.

"What?" he asks.

"He was standing." We make our way down the sidewalk. "I got a chance to look at the crime scene photos. The sand isn't disrupted in a way that would indicate he was kneeling when he was shot. The trajectory also shows the gun wasn't pointed downwards when it was shot but held straight ahead at very close range. Greg also has a few scratches on the side of his face where he hit the sand as he fell. After the gunshot. That means he was just standing there when someone walked up behind him and shot him in the back of the head."

"Not all hits have the victim kneeling," Eric points out. "It could have just as easily been an execution with him standing."

"I know that. But think about where he was. It's not like he was in the woods at night or inside a building where he could be trapped. He was found dead on the beach at the edge of the water. There was no indication he was killed somewhere else and dumped, and the time of death puts him being shot before sunset. After what he went through, Greg wouldn't just let someone march him out across the sand and then stand there while they shot him."

I shake my head, still staring straight ahead as we walk. "I need to look at the crime scene images again."

"Creagan is already pretty jumpy about this. He's not going to like you getting involved," Eric says.

I stop in the middle of the sidewalk and turn to him, stepping up close so I can stare directly into his eyes.

"Creagan can shove a flute up his ass and play *'Dixie'* with a straw. After the shit he pulled with my mother's death and dangling me like a piece of raw meat in front of a serial killer, he knows better than to get in my way right now."

Eric gives a slightly shaky nod, and I continue down the sidewalk. A few seconds later, he takes several jogging steps to catch up with me.

"When all this has settled down a bit, remind me to have you explain the physiology of what you just said," he says.

"Do you want a demonstration?" I ask.

"Not necessary. Especially if it includes visual aids."

"Then you'll just have to use your imagination," I offer.

Just as I expected, Creagan doesn't show his face as we enter the war room that has been set up to manage the investigation into Greg's murder. In the days since his body was found, a frustratingly minuscule amount of progress has been made into finding out what happened. This room contains everything investigators have uncovered, but the shreds are still scattered around, like pieces of a puzzle yet to be put together. Well, at this point, it's almost as if not just one, but several puzzles have been upended and tossed around. We have to sift through them all to even find the pieces that matter.

Some of those pieces are the crime scene photos. These photos are a sliver of time. I've always felt that crimes burn into a place, permanently altering the atmosphere. These pictures record the moment that brand is made. Even tiny details can give insight into the crime that might otherwise be lost. That's what makes them so invaluable and influential in an early investigation.

My hands pressed flat on the large oval table; I sweep my eyes over the photos spread out across it. They land on one, and I pull it toward me.

"Look," I say to Eric, running my fingertip down the trail of footprints behind Greg's body. "There are footprints all over the beach, but there wasn't much rain in the days before the murder, so the sand was dry. The footprints are shallow. They just pressed down into the very surface of the sand. But look at the ones behind Greg."

"Like the mud under Martin Phillips," Eric notes.

I nod. The deep impressions of boot marks sunk into the wet ground at the train yard, just beneath where the orderly was tied to a fence and tortured, are clear in my mind. They almost superimpose the footsteps in the picture I look at now.

"Exactly," I tell him. "Those were made when Anson picked Martin up to hang him. Some of those marks were shallower because only he was standing in that place, but then they got deeper when he lifted him up. He had to press his weight down to get leverage. This is the same idea, but not because somebody picked Greg up. Instead, Greg made footprints going across the sand up to the edge of the water. Then another person followed behind, following in his exact footprints. It made them much deeper than any other footsteps nearby."

"So, whoever shot him followed directly behind him rather than walking beside him," Eric says.

I nod.

"So, again, I don't see somebody marching Greg out across the beach in the daylight and shooting him. Greg wouldn't comply like that. There would be a fight; he would try to make a scene and get away. But if you look at the sand, there isn't any sign that he reacted at all. He walked to the edge of that water and dropped dead where he stood. No struggle. No movement like he was turning around in response to anyone," I say.

"So, why was he out there? Greg doesn't exactly strike me as the beach-going type," Eric says.

"Definitely not," I agree. "The one time I convinced him to go to the river with me, he slathered on sun factor two thousand and still sat under an umbrella the entire time with a shirt on. He was never a water person. He would hike and was a really skilled boxer. When he was a kid, he built go-karts."

"Seriously?" Eric asks.

I nod, an unexpected laugh bubbling up.

"That was his fun fact."

"His what?"

"His fun fact. We didn't have a cute or romantic story about how we started dating. It just kind of happened. But at the very beginning, when we first met, he did try to flirt with me a little. He just wasn't very good at it. He was too analytical and precise for that. We already talked a lot about work and our current lives and everything, but once he decided he was attracted to me, he just stopped being able to communicate. So, one day when he was struggling with having a conversation with me, I asked him for a fun fact about himself. It was supposed to just throw him off his game and force him to think outside the structured conversation he seemed to have planned," I explain.

"And his was about go-karts," Eric acknowledges.

I nod, looking back at the table and a picture of Greg before he ended up on that beach.

"Yes. He didn't even really have to think about it, which was pretty funny. It was almost like that was the only fun fact about him, so it was easy for him to think of. But he told me that when he was younger, he lived in a pretty rural area, and it was just a normal thing for boys to build their own go-karts. As you can imagine, he didn't have a lot in common with most of the guys in his area. But he was smart and mechanical, so that in particular really resonated with him. He was able to build impressive karts; he even entered into races with them." I glance over at Eric with a tense smile. "I bet you didn't see that coming."

"I'm just envisioning a miniature Greg in a little child-sized suit, racing go-karts," he smiles with a tinge of sadness to his voice.

The image is pretty funny; I have to admit. But I've slipped off track, letting my mind go into nostalgia and memory rather than focusing on what's in front of me. Even though Greg and I had been over for a long time before all this, it still hurts that he's gone. Shaking away the emotion, I look back at the pictures in front of me and focus again on the footsteps.

"I think he went on to the beach himself."

"What about the blonde woman on the security camera?" Eric asks.

"I don't know. It definitely looked like she at least left with him. But I don't think anybody was with him when he first walked out onto the beach. It looks like he did that on his own, and then someone came up behind him."

"Maybe getting through his captivity with Jonah and surviving being brutalized gave him a new lease on life," Eric suggests. "He could have decided he didn't want to follow the same patterns and routines he did before and was going to try new things."

I look up at him, any tiny fiber of humor that might have existed in me now gone.

"Yeah. So, he left the hospital without telling us, went to watch the sunset over the ocean, and got a bullet in the brain for it."

SIX MONTHS LATER …

The fall night is sticky and oppressive. Too hot to be October, even in Sherwood. I wake up unable to breathe. Instinct stretches my hand to the side, but I find nothingness. Sam is on duty tonight, leaving my sweaty sheets empty and still. The stifling air around me is too quiet.

It swells in my lungs rather than giving me a fresh breath. I can't force the air in.

My body feels impossibly heavy. Like I'm being pulled down into the mattress. At the same time, something aches at the very center of my being. A blast of force in my gut propels me up. Barely realizing what I'm doing, I run up into the attic.

I haven't climbed these stairs in months. My bare feet take them two at a time, nearly slipping from the edges. Fine dust on the bare wood floor feels soft on my skin. A fleeting thought goes through my mind, wondering if I'm leaving footprints. Wondering if anyone would notice.

Each second burns in my lungs. The air isn't any easier to breathe up here. There are no windows I can open. This attic was used once. Many years ago. Many people ago. In the recesses of my mind, corners I rarely venture into anymore, there are memories of that time. Of the little table that used to sit against one of the walls, adorned with a tiny lamp. It looked like an urn. Rounded white porcelain with pink Rosas painted on it. The shade had deep pleats, like the ones in my grandmother's skirts when she went to church on Wednesday nights. They were her casual skirts, the ones that brushed her calves and hung in heavy cornflower wool from the wide band at her waist.

The table isn't there anymore. Neither is the hulking armoire that used to stand against the other wall. Swallowing up the empty space as if to declare there was nothing else for this room to be. It stood in front of a part of the wall with textured wallpaper lined up perfectly. Like it had been there as long as the wall itself. But there was more to the wall behind where it once stood.

Bits of the wallpaper still speckle the floor, fallen from the long, torn pieces hanging like ripped flesh from the gaping gash in the wall. There's darkness beyond it. The door still stands open, just as I left it that day months ago. When I took an axe and smashed the facade away and uncovered all the secrets of this house.

Much of what I took out of the secret room that day and in the ones that followed is sitting in an evidence locker somewhere, waiting to be used in the ongoing trial. But there are still remnants. The shelves are still nailed into the walls. Tables still sit in corners. Some crates are scattered across the floor, with papers threatening to spill off the edges. I can't see them in the darkness, but they're there.

The floodlight Sam brought over is still sitting in the middle of the attic floor. I turn it on. White light explodes, so intense it could cut through stone, sending shadows back behind their objects. Everything is illuminated.

I step inside and look around, then reach for the nearest shelf.

Sam finds me the next morning asleep on the floor of the attic, my hands bloodied and raw, the space around me cluttered with broken shelves and crates dragged across the floor.

The room is empty.

CHAPTER ONE
NOW

"Babe?"

Sam's voice drifts up the stairs into the attic, and I stand up from where I've been hunched over painting the new baseboards in the tiny room.

"I'm up here, Sam," I call down to him and step back to look at the coat of paint.

For years I forgot this room was even here. It was one of many parts of my childhood that got so twisted and blended with questions and false memories; it stopped existing in my mind. It wasn't until I saw a similar room in the house across the street that I started questioning my memories of my grandparents' home. Pam, the representative from the property management company, mentioned the feature exists in almost every house on the street. But that only served to deepen that wedge in my memory. What was the difference between what I remembered and what was the truth?

A series of events last year brought those memories crashing down on me, and a few precise blows with an axe literally thrust them in front of my eyes. Along with long-buried secrets about my family that still linger with me.

It's taken months for me to be ready to face it like this. For a long time, I just kept pretending it wasn't there. The information sealed up behind the wall shattered my understanding of my life. Forced me to come face-to-face with horrible realities I thought might destroy me, even as they filled gaps in my understanding and answered questions I'd carried with me my whole life. After Greg's murder and the crushing investigation that followed, I simply pushed the room back out of my mind.

But even that couldn't last long. I went from not ever going into my attic and ignoring that I'd ever seen the room to tearing it apart in a split second.

I had been back in therapy for a few weeks at that point, but it wasn't doing much for me. The block against it wasn't new. From the first time Creagan funneled me into the therapist's office as a condition of continuing to work for the Bureau, I resisted. No one could possibly understand what I went through when I was younger or how it continues to impact my life even as an adult. Even I didn't fully understand it. It seemed futile to try to unpack it for someone else just so they could repeat it back to me under the guise of helping me sort through it. But I sat there. I let the therapists try to crack me open and crawl around inside to find the bits I hid.

I didn't want to go back. Everything I tried to understand the first go-round was now revealed to me. I know what happened to my mother. I know why my childhood was spent bouncing around and never really settling into one place. I know who I am. I had no interest in going over it again, or in adding Greg to the mix in a new way. I'd already talked about him. My therapist knew what I went through when he disappeared and how that played into my breakdown two years ago. I didn't want to go any deeper or talk about his death.

But I didn't have a choice. That dusty pink couch was waiting for me, and I had to fill it. But they couldn't force me to unzip my soul and spill my guts out. She could only sit there and wait. The words were mine, and I could choose when and if to say them. For those few weeks in the beginning, I barely spoke. I listened to her try to prod me along, only answering her questions with the simplest words I could, but I didn't offer her anything else. Not until October. Not until I couldn't breathe.

I slept almost the entire day after tearing the room in the attic apart. Sam gently washed my hands and wrapped them in bandages, then tucked me into bed and cared for me there until I felt like I was back in reality. The next day I walked back into my therapist's office and told her what happened.

She called it a breakthrough. I didn't care what she called it. All I knew is something shifted. I still wasn't able to come back up into the attic for a long time. Everything stayed exactly where I left it. I couldn't even go up to get the Christmas decorations or return them after the new year. But gradually, I chipped away. I brought myself through the house. To the bottom of the stairs. I opened the door. I turned on the single bulb that hung over it. Two weeks ago, I walked through the swaying light and climbed the stairs into the attic. The destruction was still there, and I put myself to the task of putting it all back together again.

The cuts on my hands are gone now, and I don't shake when I climb the stairs.

Sam comes up into the attic. I stretch my back to release the tension in the muscles. It's amazing how just crouching down to paint something as simple as a baseboard can create so much discomfort. He leans down and kisses me, putting his big strong hand right on the spot of my back that hurts. It's amazing how he can tell exactly what I need. I lean into his touch, letting the warmth of his skin sink through the baggy button-up shirt I have over my clothes.

"It's looking really good up here," he tells me. "So, I see you went with the ecru."

I look down at the section of the wall I just finished painting and narrow my eyes at him.

"That's eggshell," I tell him. "Can't you tell the difference?"

But he looks at it; his head tilted to the side.

"Seriously?" he asks.

"I actually have no idea," I smile. "It's white. I just got the first one on the shelf."

Sam laughs and shakes his head.

"Well, whatever color it is, you're doing a good job. Is the electricity still holding up?" he asks.

I reach over to the newly installed light switch and flick it up and down a few times to show off the bright bulbs that now fill the room with warm yellow light.

"Looking good. Hasn't lit any fires or anything," I shrug.

"What do you know, I do have some skills," he teases.

I turn to him for another kiss.

"You have a lot of skills."

"Is there anything else you want to get done up here? Or are you good for a break?"

I look back into the room and let out a breath.

"A break seems like a good idea. Do you have something specific in mind?" I ask.

"Maybe the giant containers of biscuits and gravy from Pearl's I have downstairs," he suggests.

"You always know just what to say," I tell him.

Sam gives me his bright, boyish smile and reaches down to take my hand so he can guide me down to the kitchen. I stop by the bathroom first to wash my hands, and by the time I get to the kitchen, he has already spread the food out and is pouring fresh coffee into a mug for me.

"What time is it?" I ask, realizing I don't even know how long I've been up in the attic.

"About three," he tells me. "Does that mean you haven't stopped since you went up there this morning?"

I accept the mug from him and take a long swallow.

"Maybe," I shrug.

"You've got to stop doing that, Emma."

"I know. I just want to get it done. It will feel so much better when I can pretend that room has always been a reading room," I say.

"Are you really going to be able to do that?" he asks.

My eyes lift to him, and the words tumble down along the back of my spine.

"Let's eat before everything gets cold," I say.

He regrets the words now hanging in the air around us. I can see it in his eyes. But I won't say anything. I'll leave them alone and hope with enough breaths; they will dilute and fade away. In, out. In, out.

As I take my first bite of intensely buttery biscuit and rich pepper gravy, I notice a stack of envelopes sitting on the corner of the counter. I nod toward them.

"What's that?" I ask.

"I brought your mail in," Sam says. "The box was getting a little full."

He doesn't elaborate, but I know he worries about how accustomed I've gotten to the walls of my house. I work with him on cases occasionally, but if I don't have the distraction of an investigation or the mind-erasing routine of a night on the beat, this is where I stay. I know these walls, and they know me. He reaches for the stack and hands it to me. I sift through some junk mail and a couple of cards and letters from former colleagues at the Bureau. They've been trickling in for months now as people come to terms with me leaving Headquarters permanently.

I always knew there was going to be a time when I was going to have to make a final decision about the FBI. Creagan walked on eggshells around me for a good while after I discovered his prior knowledge of my mother's involvement with Feathered Nest. It was a good choice on his part. He knew as well as I did that gave me leverage to make his life a living hell if I so chose. Both professionally and personally. But I focused on deciding my own future instead.

Since my first case back in Sherwood, when I was on modified leave, I always felt in the back of my mind that I would return to full duty at some point. My house was still sitting there waiting for me and I figured I'd move back eventually. The Headquarters was where I was used to being. But the longer I was away, and the more I've been through, the more obvious it's become that I can't go back to that. It was a safety hatch. A net I put under myself to make sure I always had another option. Just in case.

Just in case I couldn't bear to be back in the hometown I left behind.

Just in case I couldn't look at Sam's face and live with the choice I made.

Just in case I couldn't help being in this house, surrounded by memories of the days I spent here and the haunting thoughts of moments I never got to live.

But those fears didn't come true. It hasn't always been easy to be back here, but I can't look back. My house is still there, but now it's what it was always meant to be. My father's home. And I am now one of a little-known breed – FBI special agents living in communities and towns far away from any of the field offices.

Most people only think about the agents who are close to Headquarters in Quantico. Some others know about the field offices scattered across the country. Those offices ensure investigations involving areas that aren't close to Virginia have access to the resources, technology, and agents they need.

Then there are those of us who live away from the offices. Often very specialized, these agents aren't constantly working or out in the field. For some, such as hostage negotiators, they are brought in only during very specific situations when their individual skills are needed. For me, living in Sherwood as an agent means acting largely as a consultant and doing investigative work that can be done through research rather than leg work. Remote work means I can stay in Sherwood and stay involved in cases through video chats and email rather than having to be in the Headquarters.

When I'm needed for an in-person investigation, I travel. But that has been extremely limited over the last year. I haven't been out in the field or doing any undercover work since Greg's death. My only in-person work has been at the Headquarters and the last time that happened was several months ago. My face is still too recognizable to many people. I made too much of a splash when everything went down with my father, Anson, and Jonah, and, finally, Greg. In a rare moment of seeing eye to eye, Creagan and I agreed it would probably be best if I stayed out of the public eye for at least a little while. I couldn't risk doing an investigation and having key players immediately recognize me.

There are times when I really miss being right in the middle of all of it. Headquarters has an energy about it that I feed off of. But that's not for me anymore. My life here in Sherwood is where I'm supposed to be. It lets me work with the Bureau, help Sam when he needs me, and continue contemplating what a future might look like as a private investigator. For the first time in my life, I feel like I actually have the ability to choose my future. I don't have to be tied to my past and stay in the same place because it's the path I've been following.

Finding the answers I sought for so many years set me free. I'll never feel like I know everything. There will never be a time when I'm totally at peace over what happened. But that's something I've learned to live with. It's like the haunted energy of a place where a life was ripped away or a scar across my skin. It will always be there. Nothing will change it.

So much of it still haunts me. But it's not about my mother anymore. That part of my life, I can move on from. I'm not ready to move on from Jonah. There's too much that hasn't been explained. There are too many questions that haven't been answered and too many threats that still linger. But the feeling is different. When I started investigating my mother's death and my father's disappearance, the Bureau was there for me. They were my opportunity. With their resources and the training they could offer me, I could not only pursue the mysteries of my past, but find vengeance for others.

Now I'm not searching for that. The FBI didn't even know Leviathan existed. My father was beginning to unravel it when he disappeared. Now he is heading up the investigation within the CIA and cooperating with the FBI. But even with that, the Bureau is putting little emphasis on uncovering the full extent of the organization. Or what it might have been responsible for over the years.

It makes it even more personal. I don't need the Bureau to protect me anymore. I don't need them to guide me. When I work on cases with them, I am doing just that. Working for them. It doesn't feel like it's about me anymore. I just have to decide if that's enough for me.

CHAPTER TWO

I'm almost to the bottom of the stack of mail when I get to a thicker envelope. The rest of the mail slips from my fingers when I see the return address.

"What's wrong?" Sam frowns. "What is that?"

"It's from the probate attorney," I tell him.

Greg's murder was an incredible shock, but the aftermath threw me for even more of a loop. The days and weeks following the discovery of his body on the bloody sand were a blur of investigations and questions, trying to understand how it could possibly have happened.

He wasn't supposed to leave the hospital by himself. The incredible danger he was facing the entire time he was in the hospital was known to every person who worked in his ward. Even after Jonah and Anson were arrested, we knew that danger was still there and still had his floor on heightened security. It was going to get worse when he was released and didn't have the security and locked doors to keep him safe.

That's why he was supposed to wait. As soon as it came time for him to be discharged, it was arranged for me to pick him up at the hospital and escort him to his welcome home party and then to the secure location where he would continue his recovery. It was all planned out. The Bureau had arranged for a safe house, and he would be monitored and protected as long as it was necessary. But for some reason, he left. For some reason, he didn't wait.

When he walked out of the hospital, it was with only a blonde woman, no one recognized and who still had no name or connection. Days went by, and we still couldn't untangle this newest knot. And the realities of his death settled in.

It wasn't just coping with the reality that he was murdered. It wasn't just having to completely adjust a thought process that had already been altered long after I thought I might never see Greg again. He broke things off with me out of nowhere. Then he disappeared in an instant, and no one knew what happened to him. Then he appeared again, beaten, and brutalized, and my world became one that included him again. Not in the way it used to. It would never include him in that way again. But he was there. He was alive, and he held secrets and information critical to me being able to understand my uncle and the vicious way he destroyed my family.

Then just as quickly, he was gone once more. Only this time, it was permanent. There was nothing abstract about it now. When he went missing, I never truly let myself believe he was gone. I never talked about him in the past tense or thought about how he might have died. It's not that I had any sort of intuition, or I heard his voice at night or anything. It just never felt right to think of him as being dead when I couldn't think that way about my father after his own disappearance. There were enough people in my life who were truly gone. I could never again think of my mother as possibly being alive somewhere, and I couldn't bring myself to disrespect that by putting Greg or my father in that place.

Now I know the answer to both of those mysteries. I know my father is back in the house where he was living before he disappeared, re-assimilating himself to a more normal daily life.

And Greg is dead.

Less than two weeks after the discovery of his body, a lawyer contacted me. Jeffrey Grammer was his name. He was the last person

I expected to hear from, and the news he offered me was so shocking, so unexpected it took a few days to even fully process it: Greg had no family. None that he was close enough to for an ongoing relationship, anyway. There might have been relatives scattered around, the kind with shared blood but not shared thought. According to Mr. Grammer, who came to my house and sat at the very edge of the couch like he wanted to be able to get up and run at any second, that was the reason Greg made the decision he did.

Mr. Grammer was the executor of Greg's will. It was surreal enough to hear those words. Of course, I knew Greg had a will. That was the kind of person he was. Like my parents. Like me. Making a will is the cautious, responsible thing to do when you work in this field. It was perfectly on-brand for Greg.

But that didn't make it any easier to hear the lawyer talk about it. Hearing that was so final. More final, even, than viewing Greg's body. I could reduce his body to nothing but an object, another detail of a crime scene, just like I do with every other crime I investigate. I could make myself look past the scar on his arm that I knew came from a car accident when he was a teenager. I could make myself look past the tattoo on his thigh most people didn't know about that commemorated his father's death in the military. I could even look past the lingering signs of injuries he sustained when he was being held captive by Jonah.

All of those were just details. But the lawyer coming to my house to read his will was closing his life. There was nothing left after that. Everything he'd ever done or accomplished was now a legacy. Everything he owned was now... mine.

Except for a few specific things he left to Eric, the entire estate came to me once probate went through.

I didn't understand what the lawyer was saying when he told me that. It had to be a mistake, or I just misunderstood him. But he repeated it. He showed me the document, signed by a fully stable and functional version of Greg Bailey.

The envelope crackles under my finger as I slip it under the flap to take out the sheaf of paper inside. I've been expecting this. The lawyer told me it could take months for probate to go through, but as the months slipped further and further toward a year, I thought maybe he figured out it was a mistake. There had to be someone else. But the paper in my hands now tells me that's not the case.

"The probate is finished," I read to Sam. "The bank will transfer the funds into my account within the week, and I can claim the physical assets at my convenience." Breath streams out of my lungs as I read the paper again. "It just still feels so strange."

"His will was very clear," Sam says. "You read it yourself."

"I know," I sigh, nodding. "But that doesn't mean I understand it."

"You were important to him."

"We broke up."

"You know why."

It feels like a lifetime ago that Greg ended our relationship and then disappeared so soon after. For a long time, I wondered what happened to make him suddenly break up with me. I wouldn't let myself feel the relief that came along with the end of the relationship because nobody knew what happened to Greg. It didn't feel right to be something close to happy that the relationship was gone when he was, too. But over time, I allowed the honesty to come and the relief to settle in.

Him disappearing didn't change the time we spent together, or that I still considered him a friend. I could worry about him and fear for what might be happening to him while also being true to the reality that we weren't right for each other. That we never were.

When I found out what happened to him, that the uncle I never knew I had abducted him under false pretenses, I finally understood why a relationship that seemed to be moving along steadily ended so abruptly.

"It doesn't feel right," I reiterate.

"He knew the choice he made. You and Eric were the closest thing he had to family. When he first put his will together, he probably thought he was providing for his future wife. That's the truth. But he didn't have it changed. He didn't put in a specification. Even after waking up, he didn't try to change it. He wanted to make sure if anything happened to him, you would be taken care of. It's what he wanted," Sam tells me.

I reach across the table and stroke his cheek.

"Thank you," I say.

"For what?" he asks.

"Just thank you."

After that night in October, I haven't closed my bedroom window. Rain, snow, dipping temperatures. It has stayed open, letting me breathe. It brings in bitingly cold air as I slip out from under the comforter and tuck my feet into my slippers. Grabbing Sam's bathrobe from where he left it draped across the end of the bed, I shrug into it and wrap it tight around me. He went to sleep hours ago, but I imagine I can still feel some of his warmth in the fibers, taking away some of the chill.

Sleeplessness brings me into the office, and I sit down at the desk, opening my laptop. My fingers click over the keyboard to access the database. I don't check it as often now as I used to, but I can't stay away from it tonight. The chewing, nagging feeling in the base of my stomach makes me bring it up and read through the information carefully.

Behind me, I hear Sam walk into the office. His arms wrap around me, and he kisses my cheek.

"They're still there," he whispers. "Both of them are still there."

The prison information comes up, showing me Jonah's and Anson's mugshots and identification numbers.

I nod.

"I know."

CHAPTER THREE

"You've finished renovating the room in your attic?" my therapist asks.

"Yes," I tell her.

"How does that make you feel?" she asks.

My eyes slide over to her, and she holds up her hands as she glances down at the notes in her lap and shakes her head slightly.

"Sorry," she says. "I know you hate that question."

"Does anyone actually like it? Have you ever had a patient come in for therapy and genuinely feel better after you ask them how it makes them feel to go through the worst experiences of their lives?"

She has her mouth open like she's going to answer, then closes it and gives a slight shrug.

"Different strategies work for different patients. Sometimes, no, they don't. But sometimes patients need to actively confront and process whatever it is that's troubling them so that they can regain a sense of normalcy with themselves."

"But sometimes you just make them re-experience whatever trauma they had in the first place?"

She sighs but doesn't say anything.

"That's kind of ironic when you think about it, isn't it?"

She nods. "So, let me ask it another way. Did renovating that room do for you whatever it was that you wanted it to do?"

"I think so. Knowing all the information and reminders of my uncle were kept in there for so many years was driving me up a wall. It felt like there was a part of my house that wasn't really mine. I'll always think of that house as belonging to my grandparents, but this is different. It's like that room was completely separate from everything else. It wasn't a part of the house; it didn't belong to anything. It was stolen, in a way. Does that make sense?"

"It only matters if it makes sense to you," she says.

"Well, that's exactly how it feels. Even in all that time that I didn't go up there, I could feel it. It was looming there. This chunk of the past that made me feel sick when I thought about it. But I didn't want to get anywhere near it. All those things were hidden from me my entire life. I can understand why my grandmother wanted to keep them. No matter what Jonah did or continues to do, he was her child. He was her little boy, and no one could have imagined what he would turn into. She wanted to cling to that. Even if she could never see it or talk about it or acknowledge it even existed, she wanted to make sure somewhere in the world; there was still a part of him that she could hang on to."

"As you've told me before," my therapist notes, "you have a very strong grasp on why that room existed the way it did. But why don't you tell me more about why you wanted to change it. You could have just taken everything out, thrown it away, and sealed it back up."

"I could have. But that would have been letting him keep it. It still would have been hiding something. This way, I have that space back, and I can use it the way I want to. Nothing needs to be hidden from me anymore. I know who Jonah is and what he's done. I don't have to make guesses or try to come up with ideas about why my mother was taken from me. I got all the answers I wanted about that, so there's no need to hide from it anymore. Jonah is in jail, and he's going to spend the rest of his life in prison. He can't hurt me anymore."

"It's good to hear you say that."

"Does it sound convincing?" I ask.

"That depends on who you want to convince."

"I know both him and Anson are in custody. They're being held in maximum security and have no movement. They're not in the general population; they aren't being moved from facility to facility. Everybody is very aware of Jonah's influence and Anson's intellect. They know what these men are capable of doing and are going to every extent to keep them from doing anything. I know that."

"But?" she leads.

"But I can't get them out of my head. I can't stop thinking about what they might have planned or orchestrated that none of us know about. Jonah's managed to exist under the radar for almost thirty years without me knowing anything about him. For more than twenty of that, everybody thought he was dead. He was able to continue throughout his life, rise to the top of a terrorist organization with a reach we are still trying to get a grasp of, and build up a following of slavish devotees without the FBI, the CIA, or anyone else detecting that he did not die the night of that car accident."

Then she drops the million-dollar question.

"Do you believe Leviathan was behind Greg's death?"

It's a question I know she's been clamoring to ask me for months now. She touched on it early in my renewed course of therapy, but I closed it down. I wasn't ready to let my mind go there. But now that's where I'm standing. There isn't anywhere else to turn.

"I don't know," I admit. "Obviously, that was the prevailing theory early in the investigation. He had only just survived more than a year of captivity and a near-fatal beating at the hands of that organization. It was his survival that directly led to us uncovering the details of Leviathan and confirming its existence. His information directly led to Jonah being captured. It only made sense that the organization would be out for his blood. They lost their leader who they saw as the most powerful and important person in the world."

"Then why don't you sound convinced?"

"There wasn't enough evidence. Our understanding of Leviathan is still so basic. Even with my father back and revealing everything that he's learned about it after going deep undercover for ten years, we still don't know enough about the organization to be able to effectively trace the members, or even how the hierarchy is built. We can't figure out how to identify who is in the organization and what they're responsible for doing. It would seem that people walking around with these sea monster tattoos on their backs would be so obvious."

"You would think," she notes.

"And yet they're not. That's what's so frustrating about it. They stay undetected. They just moved about among everybody else without anybody realizing who they are or what they're capable of. Even if Greg's death was a hit in retaliation for Jonah's arrest, we can't trace it."

"It's more than that," she tells me. "It isn't just that there's no concrete evidence. You've solved crimes before where you had barely anything to go on. What are you really thinking about Leviathan's responsibility?"

My eyes narrow slightly.

"I thought I was here to work through my personal baggage. Not the investigation into Greg's death."

"We're going to talk about whatever you want to talk about," she responds coolly.

"Then let's talk about something else," I tell her.

She opens her hand to me in invitation.

"Go ahead," she says.

We spend the rest of the session dabbling into my relationship with Dean and what it's been like coming to terms with having a cousin fathered by the uncle I didn't know about. This lets our conversation drift over into what it's been like to have my father in my life again. From the beginning, I figured that would be deep analysis fodder. His disappearance has been a central part of my therapy from the first time I sat on the dusty pink couch and stared at the woman looking back at me with expectation.

It was never lost on me that she wanted me to come to terms with the probability my father was dead. She guided me right up to that point many times, but I never let her tip me over into it. It fascinated her, and now that he's surfaced again, she's eager to explore how it's affecting me.

I feel like it's a disappointment to talk about. Of course, I'm thrilled that he's back and I can pick up the phone and call him anytime I want to. That I can ask him to send me a picture and get it in a text message seconds later. I know where he is and how he's doing. With a few exceptions of when he's gone on assignments, he's been back at the house and in a life just like before he left. Little has changed between us. We don't live together, and I have ten years of memories to tell him about, but there's no discomfort. No awkwardness.

My father was always a part of my world. Only now I can hear his voice. I can see him smile. There's more gray in his hair, more lines beside his eyes. But he is still my father. Nothing has changed.

CHAPTER FOUR

My phone rings as I'm leaned over, staring at containers of yogurt. I glance at the screen and smile.

"Hey, Dean," I say, holding the phone between my shoulder and ear as I pick up two of the containers.

"What are you up to?" he asks.

"I am currently trying to determine if I am the type of woman who can eat sea salt caramel flavored yogurt," I tell him.

"Doesn't that defeat the purpose of yogurt?" he asks.

"It's Greek," I offer.

There's a brief pause.

"Does that mean anything?" he asks.

"I don't know. I think I'm going to take a walk on the wild side."

"Go for it," he says. I toss the yogurt into my cart.

"It'll be something I can talk to my therapist about at my next session," I joke.

"How's that going?" he asks.

"I mean, it's therapy. So, it's not my favorite thing in the world. But I guess it's giving me the chance to vent a little. My last session was yesterday. I've been doing most of them on video chat, but I was in town yesterday, so I actually went into the office. I don't know why, but it feels completely different actually sitting there in the room with her."

"Why were you in town? I didn't think you were on an active investigation right now." Dean says. "Were you seeing your dad?"

"No, it wasn't for an investigation. I just finished consulting on a case, but it's all remote. I saw Dad, but that wasn't why I was there. Greg's probate went through, so I was collecting his things," I explain.

"Oh," he says. "I'm—"

"Please don't say you're sorry," I cut him off. "I have heard that so many times, and I just can't hear it anymore. Everything is out of his apartment, and most of it got donated right off the bat. I'm still going through a few of the boxes, but I don't really see myself keeping much if anything. It'll be a relief when that's over."

"I haven't forgotten about him," Dean assures me. "None of us have."

"I know," I tell him.

"We're going to figure out what happened to him."

"I know," I say.

I breathe through a tense silence, pushing my cart along the too-bright grocery aisle.

"Well, what else? I feel like I haven't talked to you in forever. What's been going on in your neck of the woods?"

"Not a lot, to be honest with you. I'm technically working in the police department with Sam in between working on cases. I go with him for some of the calls and have helped with a couple of investigations over the last few months. But for the most part, I'm just home researching. Grocery shopping and game nights with Janet and Paul across the street are my big moments of excitement recently since I haven't had to travel for a case lately. I know I made the right call by telling Creagan I should stay out of potentially high profile, in-person investigations and undercover work for a while. But it's bringing up all kinds of confusion."

"What do you mean?" Dean asks.

"My whole adult life has been about investigating crimes. It's what I'm driven to do. But I'm not feeling as comfortable with it as I used to. There are times when I miss the undercover work or constantly being on the run. But when I think about it, there isn't that spark that used to be there. I feel like I got into a rut and kind of hit a wall. The whole reason I went into the FBI was to find out what happened to my mother."

"I know."

"And that's what I did. It took seventeen years of wondering. Ten years of investigating. But I finally got the answers I was looking for. And now I just wonder if that means I don't have that purpose anymore. Maybe there's supposed to be something else. I've fulfilled that mission. So, do I keep going? Or do I find out what else is ahead of me? I guess I am trying to figure out what comes next."

"You'll figure it out," he says. "I still think you need to really consider getting your private investigator's license."

"So, we could go into a family business together?" I crack with a smile.

"Something like that," he says. "If nothing else, it would be something to have in your back pocket. You might figure out something else that you want to do or decide to go back to the Bureau in a more active role in the next year or so. You might find that small-town living isn't right for you and that you want to be back in the excitement of DC. Or that you want to stay a consultant like B rather than a fully active special agent. But if you don't, being a private investigator is right up your alley," he tells me.

He's right. At least, in theory. I'm trying not to push myself into any major career decisions right now. I need to concentrate on just reconstructing my life and figuring out who I am without all the questions looming over me. But when it does come time to join a world of normalcy again, it's possible I'll find that the FBI isn't where I'm supposed to be at all. Sam often reminds me of the girl I was before I left Sherwood for the last time before entering the academy. I wanted to be an artist. My spirit was free and light, and I wasn't constantly focused on the intense, massive cases that go to the Bureau rather than more localized investigative organizations.

Maybe Dean is right. Being a private investigator may be exactly what's right for me. I can choose my own cases and won't have to deal with the red tape and exacting protocols of the Bureau. Going up against them has created friction before. It's appealing to think I could pursue more personal, smaller cases without having to deal with orders and do things at my own pace. At least to an extent.

"Speaking of which," I say, trying to redirect the conversation, "how are things with you? I don't think we've spoken since you were trying to find that father who went missing in the middle of January."

"That's a really messed up case. I'm still working on it."

"No sign of him?"

"Nothing," Dean confirms. "I have gone through every angle I can possibly think of and followed every lead that's come up. Some of them a few times. And I haven't been able to make any progress. It's like the man just evaporated."

"It can definitely feel like that," I sympathize. "But we both know that doesn't happen. There's an explanation, and I'm sure you're going to find it. You just have to keep digging. Is there anything I can help you with?"

"I actually did uncover something I wanted to run past you to see if you had any insights."

"Go ahead," I tell him.

I go back to pinning my phone between my ear and my shoulder to dig through a bin of green peppers. Tonight was calling out for stuffed peppers, so I carefully scan the bin for the ones with the perfect shape.

"Obviously, we went over his financial records and bank accounts and everything from the very beginning. That's one of the first things you do, trying to see if you can track where cards have been used or if there's been any unusual money moving out of accounts," he starts.

"Right," I say, stuffing a couple of peppers into a bag.

"And it didn't seem like there was anything unusual. Just absolutely normal transactions right up until the moment when he disappeared. All his credit cards went dark, his bank accounts hadn't been touched, there were no unusual withdrawals in the time leading up to his disappearance," Dean says.

"That's not usually a good sign," I say. "People can't function without money. Either he was somehow saving for a long time to make sure he had enough that it couldn't be traced when he left, or he doesn't need money anymore."

"That's what I thought, too. But without a body, I'm not giving up hope. So, I kept searching, and just the other day, I uncovered another bank account."

"Of his?" I ask. "Didn't anybody run his social security number and personal information to track down any additional accounts he might have?"

"Yes. That's why we thought we had all of his information. But what we didn't realize is he had opened one under a different social security number."

"Whose?" I ask.

"His wife's."

"Wait; what? You didn't tell me he's married."

"I didn't know. That wasn't part of the information given to me during the briefing. I asked the mother of his child and his family, and none of them knew either," Dean explains.

"Who is this wife? Has anyone spoken with her?" I ask, finishing selecting my peppers and spinning the bag to close it.

"No one can find her."

I pause.

"No one can find her? She's missing, too?" I ask.

"That would be easier to determine if we could find her to begin with. I was able to dig up her information from the social security number used to open the bank account. From there, I could find a marriage license and show that they got married one week before Mason went missing. But after that, it seems like she just dropped off the planet. The only problem is, she didn't exist before that either. I can't find anything about her other than her birth certificate and that marriage license. So, we don't even know where she was or what she was doing or anything. But here's the thing. That's not even the strangest part," he tells me.

"It's not?"

"No. When I found the bank account, the police requested the transaction history. Two weeks before Mason disappeared, there was a large withdrawal. A couple thousand dollars. But then two days after he got married, more than three times that amount was deposited back into the account."

"Is that what he's been using since he's been gone?"

"You would think. It would make sense. But no. That deposit is the last transaction in that account," Dean tells me.

I push my full cart toward the cash registers, taking a second to try to wrap my head around what he's telling me.

"So, this guy started a bank account at some point and put money in it, then withdrew a bunch of money. Then he married someone no one knew existed, and no one can prove exists other than being born and marrying him. Then he deposited a whole lot of money into the mysterious account and disappeared. But the money hasn't been touched," I recap.

"Exactly."

"You're right. That makes no sense."

"That's what I was afraid you'd say," he sighs.

"I promise I'll think about it and see if anything comes to mind," I tell him. "I just got to the line, though, so I'm going to run. Let me know if anything else comes up."

"I will," Dean promises. "Tell Bellamy and Eric, I say hi. I haven't had much of a chance to talk to them recently."

"Definitely. Hopefully, we'll all be able to get together sometime soon."

It's been a long time since the whole extended group has been able to spend any time together. Some of it comes from clashing busy schedules. Some comes from the tension between Bellamy and Eric that developed a few weeks after Greg died. It's all only really let go within the last few months. Things seem to have settled between them, but I don't know all the details of what happened.

I figure at some point Bellamy will probably fill me in. For now, I'm not going to mention it. All of us have more than enough to think about.

CHAPTER FIVE

I unload my groceries onto the conveyor and smile at the young man behind the cash register. It's one of those moments that really puts into perspective how far I've gotten in my life. After my birthday last year, I slipped out of my twenties and into my thirties. Now suddenly, when I see someone even just a few years younger than I am, I immediately think of them as being so young. I feel like they are in their adult years, but I am an *adult*, in italics.

"Hi, Emma," he says cheerfully.

It's not too much of a surprise, considering I heard him greet Andre Bailey by name when he went through the line ahead of me. But it is impressive he's been able to grasp the names of so many people in town already, considering he has only been working at the grocery store for the last three months.

"Hi," I say, searching for his name. "Gabriel, right?"

He nods, his infectious smile getting even wider. A shake of his head moves a thick lock of dark hair across his forehead and reveals more of his expressive hazel eyes.

"That's right," he says. "How are you doing today?"

"Doing alright," I tell him. "How about you? Getting along in Sherwood okay?"

"Absolutely," he says. "I love it here. I mean, I knew I would. I spent a lot of time here when I was younger."

"You did?" I ask. "I don't think I knew that."

"Yep. That's why I'm back here, actually. My grandmother is here. My grandfather died a couple of years ago, and her health has gotten worse. She hasn't been able to take care of herself recently, so I came to help her out. It's really good to spend time with her, and I love the town. I'm finishing the next couple of years of college with online courses so I can be here with her," he explains.

"My grandparents lived here too," I tell him. "That's how I ended up coming here when I was younger."

He grins. "What a small world."

"Not really," I say with half a laugh. "Sherwood is kind of a grandparents' town. It seems at least half the kids I knew when I was in school here ended up moving into town because this is where their grandparents were. But it does make it special. Who's your grandmother? Maybe I know her."

"Evangeline Costas?" he asks, glancing up at me as he scans my groceries over the reader.

I think about the name for a few seconds, but it doesn't ring a bell.

"It doesn't sound familiar," I tell him. "That's the thing about this town. Too small to feel like you are anonymous but too big for you to know everybody around you."

Gabriel laughs.

"I hear that. I've been trying to learn people's name, so I can say hello to them when they come in the store, but right when I think I've gotten the hang of most of the people who shop here, somebody new comes through the door, and I have to add them to the list," he chuckles.

"Well, I think you're doing a great job."

He thanks me and fills a bag with the last of my groceries. Giving him a smile, I take my bags and leave. When the weather is nice, and I only need to pick up a few things at the grocery store, I often walk from home. It's not very far, and the surroundings are beautiful, giving me a chance to think or even just relax my brain. But today it's too cold to haul my bags back to my house. I'm shivering by the time I get to the car and toss everything in the backseat.

Getting in the car, I lock the doors and take a peek in the rearview mirror. I was just standing at the side of the car, looking into the back seat. No one is there, but it's a habit I haven't been able to shake. Maybe now that I'm no longer on active duty, the compulsion will fade. Just like the compulsion that makes my eyes flicker back and forth across the sidewalks and my hands tighten around the steering wheel a little bit more every time I pause at a corner.

It's been nearly a year, I tell myself. I don't have to be this way. Getting the answers I wanted and finally hearing the door of a jail cell slam behind the man responsible for my mother's death and also the one responsible for the torment I went through was supposed to end this. Life is supposed to move forward.

But not yet.

I'm getting there. There have been definite improvements and flecks of color glimmering across the sepia wash that took over my existence in the last couple of years. But the journey hasn't ended. There's still a long path at my feet.

Pulling up in front of my house, I open the door and step out. As soon as my second foot touches the ground, I hear a scream from behind me.

"Catch me!"

Bitterly cold air fills my lungs in a sharp inhale. I whip around to press my back against the driver's door. My hand reaches for my gun just as I see two little children race across the grass of the house across the street. Their father runs after them, his head dropping back to laugh as they slip from his grasp. My heart pounds in my chest, and my hand drops away from my holster.

It's still surreal that someone actually lives in the house across the street from me. I can't walk by the living room window without glancing out and imagining it empty and hunkering, the windows dark and the rooms empty.

But all it takes is for me to close my eyes for an instant, and I can imagine those lights coming on and shadows behind the curtains.

Images of a person who shouldn't have been there. Who no one believed was. Now the house is home to a family just getting started, and the pristine lawn is studded with toys. When the father notices me he waves. Smiling past the still trembling beat of my heart, I wave back and turn to open the back door of my car.

My mind sizzles angrily as I scold myself for the intense reaction. Grabbing everything out of the seat, I head into the house and close the door behind me. It's a relief to hear the click of the deadbolt.

These walls know me, and I know them.

An hour later, I'm in the kitchen, stirring a thick combination of onions, ground beef, tomatoes, and seasonings. On the back of the stove, a pot works on building up to a boil so I can blanch the prepared green peppers waiting on the counter. My front door opens, and I know it's Sam. I expect him to come directly into the kitchen like he always does, but he doesn't. He's moving around in the front of the house. Curiosity brings me to turn down the temperature on the stove and go into the living room to find out what he's doing. I gasp as I step through the arched entryway.

Sam stands up from where he's lighting candles lined up along the coffee table. Several more have already been clustered on either end table. A potted rosebush sits on the windowsill, and I can see the golden glint of a box of chocolates sticking up from a shopping bag sagging on the couch.

He looks up at me.

"It isn't ready yet," he tells me.

"What is all this?" I ask, taking another step closer to him.

Sam grins and reaches into the bag for the box of candy. He gives me a kiss, then holds it out to me.

"Happy Valentine's Day," he says.

The greeting twists in my chest and strikes me as odd.

"But it's..."

"I know," Sam says. "Valentine's Day was a week ago."

"And we agreed not to do anything," I raise an eyebrow.

"Yes," he tells me. "I know. So, I didn't do anything on Valentine's Day. But I wanted to do something special for you. I knew this time of year was going to be especially hard for you, and I just want you to know how important you are. I love you."

He kisses me again, and I rise up on my toes just enough to press my lips against him a little harder, so the kiss lasts longer. He presses back, and I kiss him again.

"I love you, too. Thank you for all this. Even if I did spoil your preparations a little."

Sam smiles.

"That's alright. I rarely get to slip anything past you, so just getting the candles lit feels like a victory," he says.

"It will be perfect for a drink before dinner," I tell him. "I just need to add the rice to the filling, stuff the peppers, and put them in the oven."

"Let me help," he says. "That way we can get to that drink faster."

CHAPTER SIX

We don't make it to that drink until almost an hour later. I'm still reclined on the couch wearing Sam's t-shirt and curled up under a blanket when he comes back into the living room in the bathrobe that started out living at his house but migrated over here. Our nights together have started outnumbering our nights apart. He finishes pouring a glass of wine and hands it down to me, then pulls another glass from where he has it tucked under his upper arm and pours another for himself.

"The peppers look good. Just a few more minutes for the cheese to melt and get brown," he tells me.

"Good. I'm hungry," I say.

Sam sits at the end of the couch and takes a sip of his wine.

"Did you really pull your gun on the family across the street?" he asks.

I shake my head as I swallow my own sip.

"I didn't actually pull it. But I reached for it. All the little boy did was yell 'catch me', and I went into full-on defense. It's not even my service piece. I would officially be one of *those people*."

"One of those people?" he asks.

"Those armed civilians who freaks the hell out and waves their guns around to look impressive if someone sneezes," I say.

"That's not exactly a valid analogy. You are still a special agent. Just because you are stationed in Sherwood rather than near Quantico and you don't go into Headquarters every day doesn't diminish that. Not being on an active investigation at the moment doesn't make you a civilian. Even if you weren't an agent, you are still a member of the Sherwood Police Department. And even if you weren't even that, that isn't the reaction you had. You have PTSD, Emma. You're working through it. Honestly, I admire the hell out of you for being able to be as put together as you are right now. But you're still going to have moments that get to you. There will be things that set you off. It'll take time, but eventually, it will get better," he comforts me.

I look down at my glass and swirl my wine around for a few seconds, watching it cling to the sides, then slide away.

"At my therapy session yesterday, she started talking about Leviathan again. Asking me if I think they are behind Greg's death."

"She wants you to work through your frustration at the case going cold," Sam says.

"Of course I'm frustrated," I reply, sitting up and setting my glass on the table. "Don't you think I should be? I dedicated my life to solving crimes and bringing in criminals so they can't hurt anyone else. I've solved much harder, much more complicated crimes. But I can't figure out who shot my ex-boyfriend a couple hours after he walked out of a hospital. It's been a year, and I'm no closer now than I was when it happened."

"That's not your fault," Sam points out. "If it was Leviathan, it's going to be extremely difficult to prove. You know that as well as I do. They work in the shadows, and the followers are the two most dangerous things cult members can be: obsessed and anonymous. The only lead you would have to build on is Jonah, and he was in jail before Greg died."

"That's the thing, though. I don't know if it was Leviathan. I know that seems like the most obvious option, and I'll admit it was the first thing that went through my mind when we started investigating. But the longer I looked at it and the more I thought about it, the less likely it actually seems that this was a hit put out by Jonah. I think about the way he treated the two men who shot my mother. Or what he did to Greg before he dumped him in my yard."

"What do you mean?"

"It's just... smooth and seamless like a single bullet to the back of the head doesn't fit. Jonah doesn't just kill. He makes a show of it. Remember what Greg told us about the people he removed from Leviathan? They have the tattoos on their backs cut out or burned off, and they're dumped, so they look like transients or gang killings. He wouldn't want to just kill Greg for the sake of having him dead. He would want to send a message."

"But it wasn't Jonah who killed him," Sam points out. "He had already been arrested and was in jail when Greg was shot. He could have put a hit out on him and the person he chose decided to go for a more subtle approach."

"It's possible," I note. "But it still doesn't feel right. It's been almost a year. And we haven't heard anything else. No one has come after me. No one has come after you or Bellamy or Eric or Dean. No one's gone after my father. I can understand the organization being up in arms about their leader being taken down, but if they were going to kill Greg out of retaliation, they would come after us, too."

"But if his murder wasn't related to Leviathan, who would it be?" Sam asks.

"I don't know. That's where all the frustration comes in. I just don't understand why I can't figure it out. There has to be something. I have to be missing something," I say.

"You and everyone else has been working on the investigation," Sam tells me. "You can't put that on yourself. Nobody has let this go. The case is cold, but it doesn't mean it's forgotten."

The timer on the oven goes off, and I toss the blanket off my legs to go into the kitchen. Sam leans against the door and watches me pull on a pair of oven mitts and reach down to pull out the pan of bubbling peppers. Cool air rushes up the back of the shirt as it rises up, and Sam gives a little moan of appreciation. I flip my hair to the side to look at him, and he grins, pushing away from the door and heading back into the living room.

A surge of love rushes through me, the emotion heady and silly at first, then deepening until it aches in my throat and burns in my chest. Every day I'm thankful for that man. Every day I remind myself how lucky I am to have him in my life.

I came so close to not having that. Thinking it was my only option, I walked away from him when we were younger. I put my entire life behind me so I could focus completely on my career. He could have hated me. He could have found somebody else and gotten married and lived the life he always imagined, just without me in it.

But he didn't. He lived and he loved, but we found our way back to each other. Not a single day goes by that I don't thank every entity I can think of for the chance to have him. Sam is my strength without making it impossible for me to stand on my own. He's my comfort, my reassurance, my reminder of beauty and hope when my world gets dark. He's my laughter when I can't find humor and my tears when my heart is hardened too much to cry.

I've seen enough death and horror in my life to know I could survive if he was gone. My lungs would keep dragging in air and expelling it again. My heart would keep pumping blood through veins that rush it to cells because they have no other purpose. My brain would send signals and form thoughts, etch memories, sleep, and wake. I would survive.

But I certainly wouldn't live.

CHAPTER SEVEN

March comes and with it the very first signs of spring. The shift in temperature that comes with the changing of the seasons has always fascinated me. It seems there shouldn't be any difference in what a certain temperature feels like just because of the time of year, but that's not how it is.

In the fall, the chill that starts to form in the air creeps around the edges of warmth, gradually crystallizing and sharpening down into sheets of winter ice. The spring is different. It can be the exact same temperature, but the cold feels thin and fragile. The new warmth rises up from underneath, tenuous and fleeting.

Three weeks into March, the warmth is creeping up a little more every day. I still haven't quite packed away my winter clothes, but most days, a sweatshirt thrown over my t-shirt and jeans is enough. A pair of thick socks keeps a lingering chill off my toes as I reluctantly kiss Sam goodbye in the early hours of the morning. He's working a special event all weekend, which means his hours not on duty are going to be extremely slim. If I know him as well as I'm sure I do, he's going to be catching what little fragments of sleep are available to him either on a cot in the back of the station or curled under a blanket in his squad car when he doesn't have the time to get all the way there. That means I'm not going to see him until Monday.

But I won't be alone. I'm taking advantage of the days the best I can by having Bellamy visit for the weekend. It's been months since we've spent more than a couple of hours together. After her participation in Jonah's and Anson's apprehensions came to light, she got even busier at work. The Bureau always underestimated her a little. Now that they understand how valuable she is, they are putting her on more cases and getting her more involved. She says she wants nothing to do with being an agent. She doesn't want to go out into the field on a regular basis and definitely wants nothing to do with going undercover. But her consultant work is plenty to keep her constantly busy. I'm looking forward to some quality time with my best friend, even if I am already feeling a little sniffly over Sam's leaving.

I must still have that look on my face an hour later when Bellamy pulls up into the driveway. I'm outside waiting for her on my porch glider, wrapped up in a blanket and holding a mug of hot tea. She hops out of her car, looking excited, but as soon as she and her three overly stuffed duffel bags make it halfway up the sidewalk, her expression changes.

"Are you seriously pouting?" she asks.

"I am not pouting," I protest.

"Yes you are," she argues. "There is absolute pouting going on in this area."

She circles one fingertip around her eyes.

"I'm not pouting," I repeat.

"What happened to the Emma Griffin, kick ass, independent woman who didn't need a man in her life? All of a sudden, your boyfriend is gone for a couple of days, and you get all weepy over it?"

"I can still kick ass and be independent and also be in love with a man I happen to miss when he's not around. A very important authority taught me that," I fire back.

"Who's that?" she asks.

"Disney," I tell her.

Bellamy laughs.

"Alright, I'll give you that. As long as you don't suddenly start bursting into song, we'll be fine. Actually, no. You can definitely burst into song, but you have to teach me the choreography first. I don't want to be left out of anything."

I stand up with a grin and pull her into a hug.

"I promise I won't leave you out," I tell her. "I'm glad you're here."

"Me, too," she smiles. "We are long past due for a girls' night. Three of them in a row should start to lessen the deficit. Let's get inside."

Tilting my head to the side, I look at the bags in her hands.

"Is that all you packed?" I ask.

"I can never be too prepared," Bellamy says. "A very important authority taught me that, too."

"Girl Scouts?"

"Phyllis Nefler."

Laughing again, I wrap my arm around her shoulders and lead her inside. When she has unpacked everything in the guest room, Bellamy comes back into the kitchen.

"Are you hungry?" I ask. "That was a long drive for you to do so early in the morning. Did you have breakfast?"

"Not yet. I didn't know what kind of debauchery we had planned for the weekend, and didn't want to spoil my appetite," she answers.

"How does cinnamon rolls sound for debauchery?" I offer.

"Talk doughy to me," she sasses.

"Perfect," I tell her. "I'll make up a batch, and we can swing some by the station for Sam's."

Bellamy shakes her head adamantly.

"Nope," she says. "No men. You get to have phone calls and text messages, but that's it. I came down here under the promise of a weekend without boys, bras, or bad guys, and I'm holding you to it."

"I don't think we ever discussed the whole bralessness thing," I point out.

"It's understood," Bellamy insists.

"Fair enough," I shrug. "I will make a double batch, but I will put his in the freezer to bake them for him next week."

"Now we're talking," she says. "How about dinner? If we're going to really be serious about the sheer volume of gossiping and celebrity trash talk we're going to be doing over at the next three days, we need to be properly fueled for the challenge."

"We are two highly educated, self-sufficient women who have had impressive careers in the FBI, aided in the dismantling of terrorist groups and organized crime, and taken down serial killers. And what you want to do is spend our weekend together gossiping and talking trash about the highly fabricated lives of celebrities?" I ask.

"Absolutely," she replies with a glint in her eye.

"As long as we're on the same page," I agree. "What sounds good to you for dinner?"

"Let's revisit college," she suggests. "Like we used to when we were studying. We'll get a bunch of appetizers and snack foods and just spread them out to munch on all day and night."

"That sounds amazing," I grin. I walk back into the living room and get my bag. Digging in it, I pull out my wallet and hand her my customer rewards card for the grocery store along with some cash. "While I make the cinnamon rolls, you go up to the grocery store and stock up on everything we could possibly need."

She starts towards the door, but then turns back to me, holding up the card.

"Wait, doesn't everybody in Mayberry here know who you are? Is anybody going to give me any trouble over trying to use your customer card?" she asks.

I laugh.

"It's not quite that bad. But if you want to make sure next week's community newspaper isn't emblazoned with a headline about an FBI consultant getting hassled at the grocery store for identity fraud, go through the line with the young dark-haired man named Gabriel. Tell him you are my best friend, and I sent you," I tell her.

Bellamy looks at me suspiciously.

"Is this some sort of elaborate attempt at fixing me up with someone? You have your sights set on getting me paired off with some cute, sweet guy from around here, so I'll move to your sleepy little town and start popping out babies?" she asks.

I blink at her a couple of times.

"Well, Gabriel is about twenty-three, so he is a baby, and he's here taking care of his sick grandma, so... no."

"Damn. That would have been nice," Bellamy says. She looks over at me and grins. "Oh well. You know I love all that hustle and bustle and grime back in D.C. I'll get by."

"Good to know," I tell her.

Bellamy flashes me another smile and heads out on her grocery mission. She seems perfectly content, but I can't help but wonder if there was more to that joke than she is really putting on. Last year I was absolutely positive she and Eric were on the slope toward being together. I developed my close friendships with both of them separately, and for many years the two of them only really tolerated each other for my sake. Their personalities clashed, they annoyed each other professionally, and for the most part, were very poor candidates for occupying the same space.

But that all started to shift when Greg went missing. They didn't run into each other's arms or instantly bury the hatchet. It was more of a begrudging alliance, so we could all support each other.

Bellamy was never very close to Greg, but Eric was good enough friends to be Greg's emergency contact. It was when I was sent to Feathered Nest on my first undercover assignment after six months of desk duty that they really started communicating. They helped me with all the crazy twists and turns in my life over the last couple of years, gradually drifting closer. Honestly, it seemed a relationship was inevitable.

But something happened after Jonah and Anson were arrested, and Greg was murdered. Now it seems that brush with a potential future has my best friend longing for something more.

CHAPTER EIGHT

The cinnamon rolls have the whole house smelling delicious. I'm just drizzling the tops with cream cheese icing when the front door bursts open, and Bellamy comes rushing back inside. Her eyes are wide and her face flush with color.

"What is it?" I ask. "What's wrong?"

She shakes her head.

"Nothing is wrong. You won't believe what just happened," she says, sounding excited.

"You found a cute, sweet guy to sweep you off your feet so you can come be my neighbor?" I tease.

She shakes her head again.

"No," she says.

"You discovered a new flavor of bagel pizzas we've never had before?"

"No," she says, shaking her head again, a grin stretching from ear to ear.

"B, if you keep shaking your head like that, it might fall off. Just tell me what's going on."

"You won," she tells me.

I stare at her, waiting for her to continue, but she just keeps looking at me with bright eyes and an open mouth.

"Yeah," I say after a few silent seconds. "I'm definitely going to need more than that."

"You won the big sweepstakes," she clarifies.

"And I'm going to need a little bit more than that, too," I raise an eyebrow. "What are you talking about?"

She lets out a sigh of exasperation and sets the several grocery bags she's holding in each hand down on the kitchen floor. Digging in her jacket pocket, she pulls out an envelope and holds it out to me.

"The sweepstakes at the grocery store," she explains. "It's been going on for a few weeks, and you are the big winner."

"I didn't even know there was a sweepstake going on at the grocery store," I frown. "What happened?"

"I went to the store and picked out everything we could possibly want to eat, just like you said. Then I went and found the register line Gabriel was running. I told him I was there for you. You're right, he's a really nice guy and was perfectly happy to accept the card from me. I swiped it, and he got all excited and told me you won the sweepstakes. The manager came out and gave me this envelope to give you. It has all the information about your prize."

"What is it?" I ask, taking the envelope and examining it.

"You're not gonna believe it," she says with a little too much mirth in her eyes. "It's an incredible prize."

"What? A couple of free tickets to the county fair?" I set to work, opening the flaps of the envelope.

"No. Think bigger."

"I don't know, B. One of those cash gift cards for some high amount?"

"Even bigger!"

I let out an exasperated sigh and finally get the envelope open. "Just tell me what it is."

"A week-long all-expense-paid vacation for three to an exclusive island resort!"

"What?"

I pull the paper out of the envelope and read the words. My mouth falls open in shock. It's just as Bellamy said. A perfect getaway to a remote island hideaway in the Caribbean. Windsor Palms Resort, the finest in luxury and convenience, nestled on the idyllic island of Windsor Island.

"Seriously?" I ask. "That's a pretty impressive prize for a sweepstakes I didn't even know was going on."

I start toward the front door of the house, and she calls after me.

"Where are you going?"

"Up to the grocery store. I need to talk to them about this," I tell her.

Bellamy distinctly pouts the entire way to the store, obviously wanting me to share in her jubilant excitement. But something seems strange about this. I need to talk to the manager and find out exactly what it is I won. The last thing I need right about now is getting roped into a timeshare presentation at chez hotel, teetering on a tiny patch of land just enough in the water to be technically considered an island.

When we get to the grocery store, I go straight to Gabriel's line. He grins at me as he sees me approach.

"Congratulations, Emma!" he gushes. "I'm so excited for you."

"Gabriel, I don't understand what's going on. What sweepstakes are we talking about?"

"The one for customer loyalty cardholders," he explains. "There's been an information flyer up on the bulletin board at the front of the store for the last few weeks. Didn't you notice it?"

"I don't really pay attention to bulletin boards that much," I tell him.

"Let me call Gretchen," he says. "She can explain the whole thing to you."

He puts in a call to the store manager, and a few moments later, she comes down from the office. Dressed in gray slacks and a purple sweater with her salt and pepper hair styled in a neat bob, she looks elegant and confident. Her stride is one of authority and ease in her position. Even if I didn't remember her working at the store from the time I was a child, just the way she holds herself would tell me she was in charge.

"Hello, Emma," she says as she approaches. "What can I do for you today?"

"It's actually about the sweepstakes," I say.

"Ah, yes," she nods. "I hear you are our lucky winner. That's very exciting. But I thought you had all the information you needed. I gave the information with the prize details to your friend since she was the one who was using your customer card at the time."

"Yes, she gave it to me," I tell her. "But I don't really understand how I won something I didn't enter."

"Nobody needed to enter," she explains. "The Windsor Palms Resort sponsored the prize. It's on a beautiful private island in the Caribbean. Everyone with a customer loyalty card was automatically entered."

"Alright, but how did I win?" I ask.

"The contest was designed so that the winner would be selected randomly. The more you shopped, the higher your chances. It was set up so the winner would be selected sometime this week and you had a lucky day. Congratulations. Enjoy your trip!"

She smiles at me and walks away, headed for the cash register at the end of the row, where a teenage girl stares frantically at the register and waves for help.

"Satisfied?" Bellamy asks. "Can you just be excited now?"

I look down at the papers in my hand again. After the kind of luck I've had over the last couple of years, maybe I am due for a shift in the tides.

Sam agrees when I call him as soon as we get back to the house. Bellamy is placated by a still-warm cinnamon roll. I bring the phone outside to try to coax some more heat out of the sunlight while I talk to him.

"It'll be great for you," he says. "You absolutely deserve some relaxation."

"I feel like all I've been doing is relaxing," I tell him.

"Staying home is not the same thing as relaxing," he insists. "It will do you a world of good to get out of your routine and get into some new surroundings for a while. No Bureau work. No police work. Doesn't a dose of hot weather and lounging around by the ocean sound amazing to you?"

"It does," I tell him. "Especially since it's seeming like summer is going to take its sweet time getting here this year."

"I keep trying to tell you summer does not start in March," Sam replies with a laugh. "You would think after as much time as you spent in Sherwood, you'd remember that."

"My heart may be here, but my internal calendar is perpetually in Florida," I tell him.

"Then your internal calendar will be very happy with this trip. I only wish I could be there with you," he sighs.

"Wait; what? What do you mean you wish you could be there with me? Of course you'll be there," I say.

"I can't, Emma," he says.

"Why can't you?" Sadness creeps into my voice. I don't hide it.

"You said the dates for the trip are in two weeks," he points out.

"Yeah, the information says the trip is specifically for some festival that happens on the island. That's why they did the sweepstakes. Two weeks should be enough time to get ready for a vacation," I say.

"Not for me," he says. "My schedule is absolutely packed. This new investigation we just got into is really complicated. As much as I want to think it's going to be resolved in a couple of weeks, I can't guarantee that. Besides, we have our big trip planned for the holidays this year. If I'm going to have the vacation time to do that, I can't use any now. You have the time, and as much as I hate the idea of you being gone for a week and not being able to enjoy seeing you stretched out on the beach in your bathing suit, I really feel like you shouldn't waste this opportunity. You don't have to go alone. The trip is for three, right?"

"Yes," I confirm.

"Perfect. Invite Eric and Bellamy. The three of you haven't really spent any quality time together in months. And when was the last time you went anywhere together like this?" he asks.

"Never," I tell him.

"There you go. Take this as an opportunity to relax, give your brain a rest, and reconnect with your best friends. I love you. I've got to go."

Bellamy is gradually unraveling a cinnamon roll still in the pan when I get back into the kitchen. That's her signature technique. According to her, it only counts as eating a cinnamon roll if you have removed it from the pan. Anything else is just nibbling. That way she can eat her first cinnamon roll, but as long as the other one doesn't come out of the pan intact before she eats it, she doesn't have to cop to multiple rolls.

"What did he say?" she asks.

"He thinks it sounds like a really great idea for me," I say.

"It is," she agrees. "You need the time away."

"The investigations Sam is managing are really intense. I don't feel right leaving him when I could help," I tell her. "I didn't choose to be a special agent out here rather than going back to Headquarters because I can't handle investigating or because I lost my interest in criminal justice. I just can't work near Creagan or deal with that atmosphere right now. And I feel like there might be more for me. I agreed to help Sam and the PD here when I'm not on a case. That's why he deputized me. It's not fair for me to just run off and leave him in the lurch."

"Emma," she starts, setting down the piece of roll she just tore off and wiping the icing off her fingertips with a paper towel. "Listen to me. You are an incredible investigator. You were an exceptional active field agent. And you are an exceptional resident agent doing remote work. No one is questioning that. If you hadn't decided to leave Headquarters, you would be there for the next five decades; I'm fully convinced. They would not be able to pry you out, and they wouldn't want to. And now Sherwood is lucky as hell to have you help when you do. But after everything you've gone through, that needs to be the last thing on your mind right now. I know you're trying, but you aren't all the way back to being you yet."

"At some point, I'm going to have to stop riding the healing train and get back to normal life," I tell her. "Don't think I don't know that

Creagan has been purposely limiting how many cases he puts me on. Or that he's only choosing cases that aren't violent or too complicated. He's doing his best to keep me in a protective bubble. Eventually I'm going to have to either push him to put me back into full active duty, or I'm going to have to figure out something else. I can't just stay in this weird limbo forever."

"Sure, but now isn't that time. No one is pressuring you or has any expectations for you. And it's not like you don't have the money after the settlement," she points out. "You can afford to not be on constant active duty and to take the vacation time you have built up."

I will likely never believe Creagan's decision to sue the hospital on behalf of both Greg and me was anything more than a feeble attempt at starting to make amends for hiding the truth about my mother. I never would have pursued it on my own, but he insisted. The courts found the hospital responsible for their employee Martin Phillips' drugging me and putting me in the morgue, and also Greg leaving unattended after discharge. The judge ruled the hospital didn't have enough fail-safes in place and was culpable for Greg's death as well as the attack on me.

"Sam can't come," I tell her. "He's stuck here working and doesn't have any vacation time to spare."

"That doesn't stop you from getting a break," Bellamy says.

"What about you?" I asked. "You and Eric."

"What about me and Eric?" she asks, the emotion making her voice tight.

"I only meant why don't the two of you take the other spots? The trip is for three. Sam pointed out we haven't spent a lot of time together, just the three of us, in a really long time."

I'm still reluctant about this whole thing, but Bellamy's infectious attitude is starting to get to me. She's right. I could use some time away. And how better to do that than with my two best friends in the world?

CHAPTER NINE

I spend Monday waiting for Sam to come home, distracting myself by trying to get ready for the trip. I've already started packing lists and preparations and am sitting on the living room couch researching Windsor Palms Resort on my tablet when he comes inside. Dropping the tablet to the cushion beside me, I jump up to wrap my arms around his neck and kiss him.

"I missed you," I tell him.

Sam smiles and nuzzles the curve of my neck.

"Not nearly as much as I missed you," he says.

"How can you be so sure of that?" I ask, leaning back to look at him but keeping my arms in place.

"Because you had Bellamy here to entertain you. The two of you ate your body weight in junk food and probably spent the vast majority of the weekend talking and giggling. I had a bunch of sullen police officers who didn't want anything to do with the events or the training exercises, and I ate mostly fast food and cold pizza," he says.

"You're right," I tell him sympathetically. "You probably did miss me a lot more."

He laughs and dips me back for a deep, searching kiss. When he brings me back to my feet, he looks over at the sofa where my tablet landed.

"What were you looking at so seriously over there?"

"I'm researching the resort," I explain. "I'm trying to get my head wrapped around it and get ready for the whole experience."

"What do you mean?" he asks.

"I haven't been on a vacation like this in a really long time. The last time I was planning on going on a real vacation, a certain sheriff called to ask for my help with a case, and it's kind of been put off since then."

My eyes slide over to meet his as I tease him. I frequently remind him the only reason I'm back in Sherwood is because he couldn't crack a case by himself, so he had to call in a ringer. The truth is, that case was brutal and complicated. And as awkwardly as it began between us, I couldn't be happier with where it's brought us.

"All the more reason this is the perfect time for you to go," he offers. "But I want you to promise you're actually going to relax while you're on the island."

"I will," I reassure him.

"I mean actually *relax*, Emma. I want you to enjoy your trip, not spend the whole time thinking about Greg or Leviathan. No work. No investigations. No digging your fingers in cases back home. This is your chance to really rest and recuperate. And I think your therapist would really like to hear you are finally following her prescription," he tells me.

I roll my eyes as I pick my tablet up again so I can show him the website for the resort.

"Prescribing a vacation is still not medically sound," I tell him.

"And yet, here you are ready to be a good patient and follow doctor's orders," he comments. I shake my head and look down at the tablet, but Sam catches my chin and turns my face back to him. "I'm serious, Emma. Have fun. Be silly. Enjoy your time with your friends. Don't let anything follow you there."

* * * * *

Those words are still haunting me a little less than two weeks later when Sam drops me off at the airport for my flight. I turn to look at him, and he leans to rest his forehead against mine.

"You really didn't need to drive me all the way out here," I tell him. "I could have driven myself."

"I know," he says. "But I'm about to spend an entire week without you. You better believe I'm going to squeeze every minute out of the time before you leave as I can."

"Still," I say. "It's a really long drive for you to bring me here and then just turn around and go back to Sherwood."

"It's a pretty drive," he shrugs. "Besides, nowhere is ever too far if it's for you." He touches his lips to mine with a sweet kiss, and my resolve to leave almost disintegrates. Just before I tell him I can't go, he pulls back and nods toward the doors. "You better go. They're waiting for you."

I kiss him one more time before getting out of the car and handing the redcap attendant the suitcase I'm checking. I sling my bag over my shoulder and grab my duffel bag, then wave to Sam one more time.

"I love you. I'll call you when I get there," I tell him.

"You better," he grins. "I don't like the idea of you being up in the air without me there to cushion you if you fall."

"Not too late to join us," I say, lifting my eyebrows at him. "Spontaneous vacation? You could buy a whole new wardrobe when you get to the island."

My efforts to tempt Sam into throwing caution and responsibility to the wind and joining me fail. He blows me a kiss before pulling away from the curb and driving away. I watch him for a few seconds before following the attendant into the terminal. I've barely stepped inside when his words suddenly go from an annoying whisper in the back of my mind to a throbbing taunt.

"Don't let anything follow you there."

My eyes sweep through the large space of the airport, digging into the crowds and scanning faces. I catch every movement, taking note of every detail of my surroundings. Paying attention keeps me in control. It makes sure I notice if something is out of place or about to become dangerous. But I can't always tell.

It's not always obvious. People want to think of dangers lurking in the shadows and hiding away, but sometimes the most treacherous encounters are in full view and glowing in the sunlight.

"Ma'am?"

The voice beside me makes me jump. I whip around toward it. The white-haired redcap attendant looks almost as startled as I was.

"Sorry," I manage, pressing my hand to my heart. "What were you saying?"

"I was just pointing out those are the machines for you to check in for your flight," he explains, nodding forward toward a bank of computers in front of me.

"Thank you," I smile.

I dig through my bag for my ID and walk up to the nearest terminal. He sets my luggage beside me and holds up his hand to gesture to another representative.

"Jonathan here will help you the rest of the way with checking your bags," he tells me.

I offer him a tip to thank him for his help before turning my focus on the man who has stepped up to my luggage. His uniform is neat and pristine; his blond hair cut precisely. He almost looks like he would fit in better in the military than at the airport. He stands by as I go through the steps of checking in for my flight, then puts tags on my suitcase and carries it away.

I check the time and realize I'm early. Way early. Eric and Bellamy probably won't be here for almost another hour. At least it gives me the time to get through security and maybe settle in with a snack to wait.

It's a relaxing thought, but it doesn't convince my brain to stop spinning. I still feel jumpy as I make my way toward the security checkpoint, unpleasant anticipation tingling in my fingertips and along my spine. As much as I try not to, I'm waiting for something to happen. I know Jonah and Anson are in prison. Checking the database gives me real-time updates as to their status, and as of last night, neither of them have been moved or had anything change. The prosecutor also assured me I would be given plenty of notice before anything happened with either of them, including moving facilities.

But does that really mean anything? Jonah is the revered head of a sprawling, dizzyingly complex organization made up of an army of devoted followers ready to offer up their lives at his pleasure. They would offer up the lives of others without hesitation. And Anson was once one of those followers.

I'm still not entirely convinced he turned away from Jonah as much as he has claimed in the year following his arrest. Everything he did to me was for Jonah's attention. Anson said he felt Jonah had lost his grip. He wanted to prove himself smarter, more capable, and more powerful by tormenting me and bringing me down. I think he was desperate for Jonah's approval. His beloved leader didn't fawn on him the way he used to, and Anson wanted to reclaim that high.

In the end, it landed both men in tiny cells that are just the beginning of a long series of similar cells that will define their existence until their corpses can be tossed out with the trash. Or, that's the intention. I can't forget just how wide-reaching and complex their network is. They are connected to a staggering number of people from all walks of life. Both wield tremendous influence, especially Jonah. Just being in custody doesn't necessarily stop them from anything. Jonah can still easily contact people on the outside and give his commands. Anson may not have that type of sway over other members of the hierarchy, but he does have intense intelligence that could allow him to create all kinds of mayhem.

It has been a year with no sign of retaliation, but the comfort and reassurance that once brought me has faded. The more time that ticks by, the more the anticipation grows. Especially in places like this, I'm waiting for something to happen. Even more than the tearing feeling of the anticipation is the heaviness in how I look at myself. I hate feeling uncomfortable or afraid, waiting for them to strike.

I just want to get on with my life.

CHAPTER TEN

ONE YEAR AGO...

"Are you going to be alright?" Van asked.

Emma tossed her notebook and pen onto the table and set her bag on the floor beneath it. She shot a look at the other agent as she unbuttoned the front of her jacket and sat down.

"Yes," she answered.

"It's just that... this is different."

"Why is that?" she asked.

Van was getting uncomfortable. His broad shoulders flexed and moved backward like he was trying to make his chest look bigger. He bent his neck back and forth in little, subtle movements to keep away the creeping unease of her resistance. It had been a while since the two of them had worked together. The last time they were in direct contact was before her undercover assignment in Feathered Nest.

He was critical of the assignment, going to little effort to cover his disdain and opinion that obviously she wasn't capable of handling the work on her own. He made sure she knew his opinion, too. To hear him tell it, she was barely doing any work at all. From his perspective, she was just buttering up the situation. When it got down to it, and there was actual work to be done, that's when the boys from the Bureau would be called in.

The outcome of that assignment quieted him but didn't convince him of anything else. The disbelief and lack of confidence in her just turned into brooding that never went away. They hadn't worked on the same team since.

In a way, it was still hurtful to her. Van had been one of the first agents she met when she started working, and they got along. It wasn't until she got acknowledgements for her work and started getting more of the complex and important assignments that the cracks in his respect for her started to show.

He had always said they had her back, but she came to realize that didn't mean from him what it meant from others. From Van, having her back didn't mean they were behind her and were going to support her. Instead, he meant the guys were there to pick up her slack when she couldn't handle the job.

She never had to call in that favor.

"I know you've done this before. I mean, you've sat down with other criminals. But this one is... personal."

"You mean like Jake was personal?" she asked. Van stiffened. "I'm touched by your compassion," she said flatly, "but I can handle this."

He stormed out of the room, slamming the door. It rattled the doorframe, but not Emma. That reaction was nothing new. There was still a twinge of pain though. She'd once thought of Van as a friend, but it was far from the first time she encountered men, agents and otherwise, who didn't believe she could do her job without their help. The Bureau was still massively male-dominated, and she'd had to claw and fight her way through school and training just to be seen as valid and gain the respect of her peers. It didn't bother her that much. All it really did was make her more determined. It drove her harder and made her better.

She thought about what Van had said. The word 'criminal' didn't sit right with her. That's what he was, obviously, but it felt flimsy. A gossamer word that settled onto the surface of what he had done but didn't bind it up the way it deserved. That same word could be applied to a kid who slipped a bottle of soda into his jacket pocket before walking out of a convenience store or a woman who left her baby in the car while she ran into the grocery store. The same word that could be used for a drunk driver who blew through a red light and smashed into another car in an intersection, or a corporate executive skimming profits off the top. All committed crimes. All were, technically, criminals. Yet the word felt strange being applied to all of them.

And even more to the man brought into the room in shackles and pushed down into the chair across the table from her. A handcuff closed tightly around the leg of the table secured the chains linking his feet and hands, so he couldn't move far from the chair.

He looked at her with an unsettling blend of emotion in his eyes. There was anger and hurt there, but against the backdrop of rage was a veil of softness and longing, like light glowing behind the clouds in a storm.

They still looked just like hers.

"You came," Jonah said.

The tone in his voice made Emma's spine tighten, but she showed no emotion.

"What did you do?" she asked.

The sick smile melted from Jonah's face. He tilted his head to the side, looking at her like he was bewildered by the question.

"What do you mean?" he asked.

"To Greg. What did you do to him?"

"Emma," he started, the words coming out like a breath. "I thought we went over all this during my interrogation. And I believe you have a written statement from him describing his time with me."

He spoke about it with the same weight as he would a leisurely visit, and Emma had to fight to maintain control of her reaction.

"You know what I'm talking about," she said. "Three days ago. What did you do?"

"I don't understand. I was here three days ago. You know that," Jonah answered. "I don't know about anything that happened outside of these walls. You'll have to ask Greg if you think something happened."

Her hands clamped down so hard on the edge of the table; it felt like her knuckles might break. Her teeth ground down into each other until her jaw ached.

"Greg is dead," she growled.

His eyes widened slightly, and he sat back in his chair.

"Oh," he said. "I didn't know."

"Don't play that game," Emma warned. "I know you had something to do with it."

"I didn't," Jonah said. "I didn't even know about his death. How did it happen?"

"You tell me," she told him.

"Emma, I'm telling you the truth. Whatever might have happened to Greg wasn't me. I had nothing to do with it."

"You're trying to tell me you did everything you could to kill him before dumping him in my yard, you went to the hospital to lurk over him, but I'm supposed to believe that he was murdered within a few hours of finally being discharged from the hospital and you didn't have anything to do with it?"

"It's the truth. I have no reason to lie to you," he insisted.

Emma scoffed.

"Because that's so out of your character? It's so far out of the scope of reality that you would lie about killing a man you already lied to in order to get him to trust you, and then nearly killed him? I'm supposed to believe a man who faked his death twenty years ago after raping a woman and attempting to kidnap her child?" Emma asked.

His hands slammed down onto the table in front of him, and for an instant, his eyes flashed red.

"I didn't rape her. Mariya loved me. We were supposed to be together."

Emma's eyes drilled into him, not betraying any emotion. Waiting for him to admit to it in his angered state.

But just as quickly as the rage took over him, it disappeared, and Jonah sat back again. "I am not lying to you, Emma. I have been forthcoming and open since my arrest. You already know about Levi and Thomas. The information Greg gave you was enough to reveal several other deaths, and Fisher's actions have links to me as well. I'm going down for all of those. There's nothing to save at this point. I have no leverage. Given the irrefutable proof of the things I did, there's no prosecutor in the world who would give me a deal to reduce my sentence merely to get details of one more murder. And one more murder tacked onto me isn't going to complicate my life any further."

"But it would leave people questioning, which you love," Emma said.

A smile, more sinister than the one before it, slid onto his lips as he leaned forward toward her.

"Think of everything I've done, Emma," he said, his voice almost a hissing whisper. "No one has linked my actions to me before. Not because I hid them, but because no one has been smart enough to figure it out. I take pride in what I do. Nurturing chaos will save the world and give all who live in it purpose for existence."

He sat back. "I won't say I'm not glad Greg is dead. But he was such a waste. Things could have been so good."

Emma got to her feet as the hope rose in his eyes again, and he reached his hands toward her.

"No," she said.

"But they could have been. He could have had so much power. And you. You, Emma. You could have lived a life you could never imagine. I want to give you that life. All of us together, me, you, your brother…"

She held up a hand to stop him.

"Dean is not my brother. He is my cousin. My mother knew what you are and went to the doctor as soon as she realized the depths of your disgusting derangement."

"Please, just listen to me."

"I don't want to hear it."

She stalked out of the room, leaving Jonah locked to the table and staring after her.

CHAPTER ELEVEN

Now

At first, I think the plane must have hit a rough patch of air, and the shaking I feel is turbulence. But I'm going side to side rather than up and down, and as I get more awake, I hear Bellamy's voice coming at me.

"Emma, wake up. We're getting ready to land."

I peel the sleep mask back from over my eyes and peer around. Everyone is doing the shifting around that happens right before a plane lowers back to the ground. The passengers who made themselves at home and scattered their belongings across every available surface scoop them up to shove them back in their bags. People who didn't take a single thing out of their bags suddenly become concerned something slipped out and start searching around. Women check their makeup to make sure the travel didn't melt it off, and men comb at their hair with their fingertips to try to get it back in place from where resting against windows, and seat backs messed it up. It's the process of transitioning back from the suspended reality of travel to the real world.

Taking my mask off, I stuff it into my bag and sweep my hand through my hair. My phone and a paperback I barely opened joining the mask, I secure my seatbelt, and I'm ready for landing.

"That took it right out of you, huh?" Bellamy asks.

"You were out like a light before the snacks even came by," Eric adds from the aisle seat.

I nod, letting out the last remnants of sleep with a yawn.

"I haven't been getting the best sleep at home," I admit. "Being on the plane helped."

"Because of the movement?" Bellamy asks.

"Because no one can get in," I say. "People might complain about all the security measures and having to show fourteen types of ID, your blood type, and your family lineage to get onto a plane these days, but I'm more than happy about it. At least I know there's a record of every person on here, and no one could just follow me on board. And if someone did happen to try something, it's a contained space so they wouldn't be able to get away."

Bellamy shifts to press her back against the seat and stare straight ahead, her hands clamping around the ends of the armrests.

"Well, let's just sketch that onto a postcard. First vacation memories," she mutters.

I know the thought makes her uncomfortable, but it's the truth. Being contained on the airplane six miles above the ground gave me a sense of control and security I don't have when I'm at home. I can take care of myself, of course, but after way too many close calls over the last couple of years, I don't like taking any risks.

Sam makes me feel safe, and when he's there with me, I'm not worried about myself. I believe he would never let anything happen to me if he had any way of stopping it, and he would do anything to protect me. I want to protect him. It's the fear that something will happen to him that keeps me from being truly relaxed and at ease at night at home.

I know full well that his being associated with me puts him in danger. Just the fact that he is in my life creates risk for him, and I hate that. I can't bear the thought that something might happen to him because of his connection to me. Things are going so well between us, and he is more precious to me than I ever knew. He has already suffered because of his relationship with me. There are still scars on his back, and he deals with chronic pain in his hip from being hit by a car when I got too close to unraveling the truth behind a cult. I'm always afraid something more will happen to him.

The plane lands smoothly, and when we exit into the small airport, we see a man standing off to the side, holding a sign with our names on it. I smile at him as we walk up to him

"Hi," I say. "I'm Emma Griffin."

Impossibly straight, white teeth beam out at me from a massive smile.

"Welcome to Windsor Island. I'm Joshua. Good to meet you, Miss Griffin," he says, an accent I can't exactly place lilting his voice. "And these must be your friends."

"Yes. This is Bellamy, and this is Eric."

"Alright then. Now that I've collected you, let's get you to the resort," he says and starts toward the door.

"We need to pick up our luggage," I tell him.

He shakes his head, almost laughing.

"No, no. That's already been taken care of for you. Everything is taken care of. Come now. Windsor Palms Resort awaits you."

We follow Joshua outside to a sleek white car, and he helps us load our carry-ons into the trunk. The already blasting air conditioner is blissful, even after the short walk through the blistering island heat.

"I can't wait to get into the pool," Bellamy says, leaning her head back and pulling the neckline of her shirt away to let some of the air on to her chest.

Joshua chuckles from the driver's seat.

"Don't worry. It feels much cooler down by the water. The beautiful breezes and lush grounds make the resort very comfortable," he tells us.

The drive to the resort is long and meandering, and I quickly realize why the airport is so small. There doesn't seem to be anything else on the island. We see no other businesses or houses. The only structures that show up among the trees and dense, beautiful greenery look like gazebos or greenhouses.

"Is the resort the only thing on the island?" I ask.

Joshua looks at me through the rearview mirror and nods.

"That's it," he says. "It was a private island, and Mr. Windsor, the owner, wanted to keep it that way even after he opened the resort. He wants all his guests to feel like they have the run of the island. Of course, there are a few places where guests shouldn't go."

"Oh?" I ask.

"There are mysteries on the island," he tells me. "Legends. This island had been uninhabited for hundreds of years. But they say that long ago, people lived here on this island. But they upset the ocean spirit. People ventured into the water and down into the caves and never came back. If you look out into the water and come out onto the rocks when the moon is just right, you may see the ocean spirits. We only have to hope they are satisfied and don't get angry again."

I wait for his booming laugh, but it doesn't come. A few seconds later, the narrow road we've been following widens, and I get my first glimpse of the resort. Surrounded by tropical flowers and elaborate fountains, it looks like a painting, almost too beautiful to actually exist. Bellamy gasps beside me, and when I glance over at her, I notice Eric slide a look in her direction.

Attendants are waiting for us when we step out of the car, and Joshua hands them our carry-ons. A man in a pale gray suit greets us with a wide smile and outstretched hands. There are the beginning traces of white flecked through his dark hair, but his brown eyes are warm and inviting.

"Welcome," he says. "We've been expecting you. I am Alonso Ordoñez, one of the managers of Windsor Palms Resort. Please, let me show you to the reception desk."

I follow him through automatic glass doors into the lavish lobby. A waterfall tumbles down a rock wall in the middle of the space while huge skylights flood the area with light. Gatherings of plush furniture arranged throughout the lobby invite guests to relax and socialize, which several are doing. The atmosphere and energy of the resort is breezy and carefree, but the carefully orchestrated transportation and service tells me there are strict, complex protocols happening behind the scenes to maintain that feeling for the guests.

The woman at the desk smiles as Alonso walks up to her and introduces us.

"Welcome to Windsor Palms," she says. "My name is Constance. Congratulations on winning your stay here."

"Thank you," I tell her.

"Is there anything I can do right now to ensure your trip is everything you hoped for? Any special requests I may be able to fulfill for you?" she asks.

"Not that I can think of," I tell her.

Bellamy and Eric nod their agreement.

"Then I will have the attendants bring you to your rooms. Your luggage is already waiting for you there. If you can think of anything you may like, please don't hesitate to get in touch with me. I am a simple phone call away," she says, then gestures for the three men holding our carry-on bags.

"Thank you," I tell her again and fall into step behind the man carrying my bags.

The three men lead us along a hallway leading away from the lobby to a door that brings us into a breezeway. We follow them along a path weaving through trees and plants that make the air thick with a fresh, sweet scent. The greenery ends, and we see the pristine beach and blue ocean a few hundred feet away at the bottom of a slight grassy slope beside the path.

We make it to the guest building and ride a fast, smooth elevator several floors up before being taken to our separate rooms. The attendant uses the key Constance gave him to unlock the door, then steps aside so I can walk in.

"Your luggage is in the bedroom," he tells me, gesturing to one side of the room. "The pool is at the end of the building. Meals are available in the lobby or can be delivered to your room. Cocktails are served in the lobby every evening. Please let me know if there is anything I can do for you."

"Thank you very much," I tell him.

He leaves with a tip in hand, and I step up to the glass door leading out onto the balcony to admire the incredible view. Only when I release the latch and grasp the handle to open the door, it won't move.

CHAPTER TWELVE

I'm still shaking the handle on the balcony door when the door to the room opens.

"Oh, I'm sorry," a voice says behind me.

I turn around and see a beautiful woman in her late teens or early twenties standing just inside the door, an armful of towels held in front of her. Her crisp uniform tells me she works for the resort, and the light in her eyes speaks to hope and life. I shake my head.

"It's okay," I say. "Come on in."

She takes another few steps in and closes the door behind her.

"I'm just bringing fresh towels," she explains. "I didn't realize you'd already checked in." She tilts her head to look around me at the door. "Are you having trouble with the handle?"

I look at my hand still wrapped around the metal and give a short laugh.

"Yes, I am. It doesn't seem to want to work," I tell her.

She sets the towels down on the back of a couch and comes toward me with a friendly smile.

"Don't worry," she says. "It's not just you. Some of these doors are a little tricky. It seems there was trouble when they were installing them." She gives me a secretive look out of the corner of her eye. "But you didn't hear that from me."

"Of course not," I nod.

"You see, the doors are positioned just slightly off, so they sometimes get caught and latch incorrectly. It makes them very easy to open. That includes from the balcony. Since the balconies can't be accessed through anything but the rooms themselves, it's not too much of a problem, but it can be frustrating when they don't stay fully shut from the inside. Many guests leave their doors open all the time, so they may not notice the issue. But those of us who close them in between guests rather than leaving them open have a trick."

She shows me a small piece of metal bent and positioned toward the bottom of the door to keep it in place. A flick of her finger releases the piece, and she gestures to the handle. I barely pull on the door, and it slides open.

"Oh," I say, surprised by it gliding open.

"See? We are working on getting these doors replaced, but since there haven't been any guest complaints, it hasn't been a priority. The resort is still fairly new, so Mr. Windsor seems to discover new things he wants to change and improve just about every day."

"The owner is on the property regularly?" I ask.

"No," she shakes her head. "Not regularly. But he comes in occasionally. I've worked here for three months and have only seen him twice. He is very kind though. He made it a point to stop and talk to each of us. Treated us like people."

That comment strikes me. "Like people? I mean... aren't you?"

She picks up the towels and smooths them over her arm again.

"You might not think so, the way some of the people around here treat us."

"The guests?" I ask, hating the way her eyes darken just a little when she talks about it.

"Most of our guests are... very rich. They like to throw their money around and think it can buy them anything they want, including the ability to treat anyone however they want to. They see the people who work here as less than them and aren't afraid to show it." She suddenly looks embarrassed, like she just realized what she was saying. She covers her eyes with her hand and shakes her head. "I'm so sorry. I shouldn't be saying things like that to you."

"No," I tell her, reaching my hand out to stop her before she can walk away. "Don't worry about it. I didn't pay for my stay here, so you don't need to count me among them. And even if I did, I'd never be that way."

She smiles, her shoulders relaxing.

"Thank you," she says.

"I'm Emma," I tell her.

"Graciela," she introduces herself. "It's nice to meet you."

"You, too," I smile.

Someone knocks on the door, and Graciela looks at me as if for confirmation. I nod at her, and she steps back to open the door. Bellamy comes in, already changed from the clothes she wore on the plane to a floral dress that flows down to the metallic gold sandals that show off her perfect pedicure. Large brown sunglasses I won't tell her make her look like a fly are flipped up onto the top of her head, and she looks me up and down.

"You're still dressed," she observes.

"Should I not be?" I ask, raising my eyebrows at her.

"I'll put these in the bathroom for you," Graciela says.

"Oh, Graciela, this is my best friend, Bellamy. She's here at the resort with me and our other best friend, Eric. B, this is Graciela."

The two women exchange pleasantries, and Graciela disappears into the bathroom.

"I thought we were going to go down to the pool," Bellamy says.

"Right now? We just got here," I raise an eyebrow.

"Is there some sort of time limit like there is with eating? You shouldn't swim thirty minutes after eating or traveling?" she asks. "Come on. We are wasting precious island time."

"I just wasn't up on the itinerary," I tell her. "Give me a minute, and I will change."

Graciela gives me a knowing look as she slips out of the bathroom and heads to the door to the room.

"If you need anything," she starts, and I nod.

"I'll let you know," I tell her. "Thank you again."

"Absolutely. Enjoy your swim."

Bellamy follows me into the bedroom, and I dig my bathing suit out of my suitcase.

"You haven't even unpacked yet?" she asks.

"How can you possibly have unpacked and changed by now?" I ask.

"I'm efficient at vacationing," Bellamy offers.

"I've only managed to get in the room and learn how to open the balcony door," I tell her. "But I'll catch up."

With my hair twisted up on top of my head, my feet feeling happily freed from socks in a pair of flip-flops, and wearing a dress similar to Bellamy's over my bathing suit, I walk with her down to the brick path we followed from the lobby. Eric is already waiting there; his head tucked down as his thumbs fly across his phone screen. Bellamy reaches out and plants her hand right on top of the screen, forcing him to look up.

"Absolutely not. Phones do not exist on the island," she says.

"There's a horror movie tagline for you," I mutter under my breath.

"They most certainly do exist," Eric counters, pulling his phone out from under her hand and holding it up to her. "As evidenced here."

"Let me rephrase. We aren't using our phones while we're on *vacation*." She puts her arms around both our shoulders to start steering us down the path toward the opposite end of the building. "We are here for relaxation and to enjoy the splendors of nature."

"So, let's go take a dip in a cement hole full of highly chlorinated water," he comments.

We pause, and she turns scolding eyes toward him.

"I'm going to have to ask you to drop your attitude," she says calmly. "Windsor Island is a happy place, and we don't take shit like that around here."

I'm laughing so hard I almost don't notice how hard the sun is making my eyes squint. Realizing my sunglasses aren't on top of my head, I turn back.

"Meet me there. I forgot my sunglasses."

Bellamy waves, and they continue on their way as I jog back to the door. Just before going inside, I glance back to them and notice Eric subtly sway to the side, bumping her with his shoulder and hip. Bellamy giggles, and the little bit of suspicion in the back of my mind grows.

The quick clandestine text I'm sending Sam to let him know about Bellamy's communication embargo distracts me enough that I'm almost around the corner to the elevators before I notice the voices. I stop when the distinct feeling that I'm not supposed to overhear the conversation settles into my stomach. Stepping closer to the wall, I listen.

"Mr. Coltrane has requested cabin three tonight," a voice I recognize says in a tone just slightly lower than a normal conversational volume. "Please make sure it's ready for him."

"Yes, sir," a young woman's voice replies.

"And Rosa, be sure you are punctual this time. Mr. Coltrane is an important client with very high expectations. See to it they are satisfied when he arrives."

"Yes, sir."

I hurry back to the door and pretend like I'm just walking in as a man turns the corner from the elevators. He's looking down straightening the cuff of one sleeve, but I recognize him as Alonso, the manager who greeted us at the door. We're almost meeting in the middle of the space when he looks up and flashes me a grin.

"Miss Griffin," he says. "I see you've settled in. Is everything to your satisfaction?"

"Everything is very nice," I tell him. "My friends and I are just getting ready to take a swim, but I forgot my sunglasses in my bag."

"You wouldn't want that. The island sun can get very intense."

We standoff for a still second before I step around him.

"Well, they're waiting for me, so I better hurry."

"Enjoy your swim, Miss Griffin. And if there is anything I can do for you, please let me know."

I'm strangely relieved when the elevator doors close, and the floor begins to lift.

CHAPTER THIRTEEN

"It sounds like they're just trying to be really attentive and offer exceptional customer service," Sam offers later after I tell him about the encounter with the manager.

I'm sitting amidst a cloud of bubbles in the deepest bathtub I've ever seen, soaking away the chlorine and thick coating of sunscreen from the afternoon by the pool.

"That's probably exactly what it is," I agree. "There's just something strange about everybody I talk to saying the same thing. But it's even different coming from him. It's almost like he's waiting for me to want something. Does that make sense? Like he's expecting me to ask for something."

"That's his job," Sam points out. "He's the manager of the hotel. He's supposed to find out if guests want something and then figure out how to make it happen."

I let out a sigh that ruffles the pile of bubbles in front of me.

"You're right," I say. "I'm just still on edge. It's really gorgeous here. You should see Bellamy. She is in her element. We might have found her natural habitat."

Sam laughs.

"What's it like there?"

"A Barbie playset," I tell him. He laughs again. "I'm serious. It's perfect. Everything is perfect. Exactly what comes to mind when you think of 'tropical paradise,' that's it. The resort is the only thing on the island. We talked to a few of the other guests, and they said the rest of the island is just hiking trails and waterfalls. There are some gazebos around to relax in, and a couple of greenhouses of local flowers, fruits, and vegetables that are actually used for the meals served here. The only people who live on the island are the ones who work at the resort, and they have their own little village on the grounds. It's beautiful. Everything is beautiful. The resort, the plants, the people."

"Why do I feel like you don't necessarily mean that in a good way?" he asks.

"It's the people," I say. "Don't get me wrong, some of the other guests we spoke to were really nice. A couple of them say they have been coming here for the last couple of years, ever since it opened. but there are others who... aren't exactly my idea of pleasant. I'll put it that way. They are all young and beautiful and obviously extremely wealthy and used to all the perks that come along with that. The housekeeper taking care of my room even mentioned that some of them are really awful to the staff."

"That's not good," Sam says. Even through the phone, I can hear his furrowed brow and frown.

"No, it's not," I agree. "But she's a sweetheart. Everybody who works here seems to be great. They all bend over backwards to make sure things are exactly the way we expect them to be. It might be a little much for me, but I can see how a lot of people would just lap it up."

"Like Bellamy?" he asks.

"Exactly," I laugh. "She draped out by that pool like the sun was feeding her."

"And you?" he asks.

"The sun does not feed me. I floated around in my thick candy coating of sunscreen and ate the fruit out of all the cocktails the waiters brought to all three of us."

"That's my girl. But I meant, are you having fun?"

"Getting there. I haven't been in a pool in a while, so that was nice. Maybe I just need to get into the groove. Figure out what relaxing and having fun are again," I tell him.

"Stick with Bellamy. She'll remind you," Sam suggests.

"She probably has the entire week planned out already. Speaking of which, she's probably waiting for me. We're going down to the lobby for dinner. And you know I'm not supposed to be on the phone," I tell him.

"I like sneaking around talking to you. It's like we're teenagers hiding under the covers, so our parents don't know we're still up," he teases.

"I will hide under the covers with you any day."

"That's the plan for when you get home. I miss you."

"Miss you, too."

I'm off the phone, dressed, and downstairs in record time, but Bellamy is still waiting for me with an impatient expression on her face. She's ready for the evening with fresh makeup, styled hair, and a dress that accentuates her long figure.

"Where were you?" she asks.

"Did you get the room with the time converter or something?" I ask. "How can you possibly be that put together in that amount of time?" I hold up my hand to stop her before she answers. "Never mind. You're an efficient vacationer. Where's Eric?"

"Taking his sweet time too," she answers.

Her eyes shift to the side, and I follow them to notice two guys a few years younger than us looking back over their shoulders at her as they walk past. Just as they are out of sight, a man a bit older comes down the path and makes no qualms about looking Bellamy up and down before continuing.

"How does that feel?" I ask.

"What do you mean?" she asks.

"Knowing all you have to do is stand, and men will fall over themselves for you," I answer.

She rolls her eyes.

"Emma, you're gorgeous, and you know it. You see the way Sam looks at you."

"I do, that's not what I'm talking about, though. In a span of about fourteen seconds, you had three men drooling over you, and you're standing there with resting sea witch face because Eric is late."

"You're just noticing it because it's a condensed environment. A lot more guys around than usual," she argues.

I glance around at the people milling around the resort, some head to the lobby for dinner and others make their way back toward the guest rooms or down onto the sand.

"There do seem to be a lot of guys here. I've been noticing that."

Bellamy shrugs.

"It's an island. If girls are running around low on both inhibitions and clothing, the men will flock." She looks back to the building and throws her hands up. "There he is. Come on; I'm starving."

In the middle of the night, I wake up with my heart pounding hard enough in my chest for me to feel the reverberations to the tips of my toes and through the top of my head. My throat feels dry, and my bottom lip stings where I've bitten down into it. My eyes flick frantically around the room, trying to make sense out of the shapes in the darkness. Shadows stretch and condense, molding and morphing into monsters and nothingness. Finally, my brain snaps the rest of the way into consciousness, and I drop back down into the pillow.

My nightmares have followed me.

I try to close my eyes and will myself back to sleep, but every nerve and fiber of my being is crackling with alertness. I toss and turn and pull the pillow over my head, but it's no use. Finally, I get up and slip into the white satin robe hanging from the back of the bathroom door.

Crossing the room to the balcony, I do the trick Graciela taught me and step out into the cooler night air. The humidity is gone, and the breeze that carries the scent of night-blooming flowers and ripening fruit is soft against my skin. I lean against the banister and look out over the grounds of the resort below.

My room has a beautiful view of the ocean. I watch the waves shift back and forth under the moonlight for a few moments before my attention is drawn down to the people still roaming around. It's well past midnight, but they don't seem to notice. Couples cozied up close to each other walk along the brick path and down the grassy slope into the sand. Solitary men walk faster, their strides more driven and determined. Some head in the direction of the lobby, and others walk away from the guest building, perhaps toward the pool.

I'm about to go back inside for a drink when I see someone rush out of the shadows near the building. Even from a distance, I can see it's Graciela. A second later, a man follows her and reaches out to put his hand on her shoulder. She turns to him, and he steps up close. I think he's going to kiss her, but instead, they share a few close exchanges before she rushes away. The man, who isn't dressed like a member of the staff, but rather a guest at the resort, puts his hands on his hips and hangs his head for a few seconds before walking swiftly away.

Thinking over the exchange, I go back into my room and pour myself a glass of the fresh fruit juice I found in the tiny refrigerator after checking in. A little note attached to the pitcher invited me to enjoy the juice of the local fruit harvested right on the grounds of the resort and promised new flavors each day.

I bring the juice along with a lightweight blanket from the foot of the bed and my book back out onto the balcony, curl up on the chaise lounge, and stare out over the ocean to wait for sunrise.

CHAPTER FOURTEEN

At some point during the wee hours of the morning, I managed to drift back off to sleep. I wake up to the sound of birds calling and waves crashing on the beach below. The fresh air fills my lungs as I stretch out down the length of the chaise lounge and look up at a morning sky just starting to turn blue. There is precisely one cloud on the horizon, big and puffy, and the rest is bright and clear. Sunny skies indeed.

Through the open balcony door, I hear something in my room, and when I look back through the glass, I see Graciela slip quietly inside. She has her head down as she tucks the key card into the pocket of her apron and quickly moves her hand to support the tray she's balancing on her opposite forearm.

"You're here early," I note, standing up from the chaise lounge and stepping into the doorway.

She startles and grabs onto the new pitcher of juice to prevent it from toppling off the tray.

"Oh," she exclaims. "You're up."

"I'm sorry," I say. "I didn't mean to surprise you... again."

"It's fine," she says. "I should expect you to be in your own room. I just didn't think you would be up this early."

"I didn't think you would be coming in this early," I tell her. "How do you clean rooms when people are still asleep?"

She smiles.

"I don't start cleaning the rooms until later," she explains. "This early, I just come by to leave your juice and pick up any dishes from the night before." She settles the tray down onto a nearby table. "But I'm not the earliest one to come by."

She reaches down and scoops something up off the floor, holding it out to me.

"What's that?" I ask, walking toward her to take it.

"The menu for the day," she says. "A new one is slipped under your door every morning, so you know whether you want to go to the lobby or order in."

I look down at the paper, scanning my options. "That's nice."

She looks around me to the open balcony door.

"Did you sleep outside last night?" she asks.

I glanced over and laugh.

"Technically, I guess I did. But not on purpose. I woke up in the middle of the night and couldn't go back to sleep, so I just went out there to get some air. Apparently, that's exactly what I needed to go back to sleep."

"The fresh air is good for you," she comments. "I've always loved ocean air."

"Is that why you were taking a walk with that gentleman last night?" I ask, lifting my eyes curiously.

Graciela gives me a curious look as she pours a glass of juice and offers it out to me.

"What gentleman?" she asks.

"When I was out on the balcony, I looked down and noticed you talking with somebody. You kind of rushed off away from him but you were definitely in a conversation."

She shakes her head. "I wasn't out last night. I had a headache after finishing my duties for the day and went back to my room without even eating dinner. That's where I was right up until I left for work this morning."

"Are you sure?" I frown. "It really looked like you."

"No," she says. "It must have been someone else. What did the man look like?"

"He was dressed nicely. Tall. Dark skin, short hair," I describe. "It was late, so I couldn't really see a lot of features."

"You said dressed nicely. So, he wasn't wearing a uniform like a member of the staff?" she asks.

"No," I say. "He was dressed like one of the guests."

"Oh," she shrugs, smiling and shaking her head as she heads into the bedroom. "No. Staff members are all required to wear their uniform any time we're on resort grounds other than in the staff village."

"So, maybe it wasn't a member of the staff."

"A guest?" she asks, sounding almost shocked by the suggestion, then starts moving pillows to the side so she can strip the bed. "Definitely not. Staff and guests aren't allowed to— socialize— after hours."

It's a delicate way of saying 'hands off'.

I'm not convinced. I'm sure it was her I saw walking on the path in the middle of the night, but she's obviously not going to admit to it. If personal relationships with the guests are against the rules, she might be reluctant to let on. I decide to drop it but am still curious about the policies.

"What would happen if a member of the staff did socialize with a guest?" I ask, remembering the other couplings I saw last night and wondering if any of them could have been sneaking around.

"Biggest rule you can break. You'd get fired right away," she says adamantly. "Of course, nothing would happen to the guest. Nothing ever can happen to the guests."

"And you strike me as not wanting to risk that," I say with a smile.

She yanks the sheets off the bed and balls them up before tossing them aside.

"Definitely not. Getting this job has been a dream," she tells me. "I have three brothers and four sisters back home. My mother always told me I shouldn't settle for anything, that I should always push for my dreams. When I first found out about the opportunity here, I didn't know if I wanted to do it because it would mean leaving my family. Coming all the way out here where I didn't know anyone and couldn't help around the house didn't seem right. But then Mama reminded me my life was mine. That I needed to do what was right for me. Going after this would show my siblings that we weren't defined by anything, and we didn't have to let anything stop us. The whole world is out there, and all we have to do is be willing to chase it."

"That's amazing," I say. "How did you find out about this place?"

"They were advertising, looking for new staff. They offered room and board, activities, benefits, and still excellent pay for me to send money home to my family. I applied and within just a couple of days, did an interview over the computer, was hired, and they whisked me off to here. It was all such a whirlwind I barely felt like I could catch my breath."

"And you've enjoyed working here?" I ask.

"It's been wonderful, for the most part."

"You mean other than the obnoxious guests?" I ask.

She looks over her shoulder at me and smiles.

"Other than that," she confirms. "It really has been, though. Windsor Island is so beautiful. On my days off, I explore with some of the other girls. There's always something new to find, something we haven't seen. Some of the people who work here come from other nearby islands, and they tell us stories. Everything is taken care of for me, and Mr. Windsor treats us well. It's not easy work, I won't say that, but for everything I get out of it, it is absolutely worth it."

"I'm sure your mother and siblings are proud of you," I say.

"Thank you," Graciela says, reaching down to gather up the bedding. "I'll get your fresh things."

I don't think about the conversation much more until later that morning when the three of us are walking back from breakfast. Ahead of us, beyond the area of the path enclosed by the plants and trees, I notice the man I know I saw talking to Graciela last night. He's walking down the path again, but this time his stride doesn't have the same intensity or determination that it did when he was walking away from her. He pauses in front of the guest building and glances over like he's looking at someone on the beach. With a quick turn of his head every which way, he steps off the path into the grass and heads down toward the sand.

"Where are you going?" Bellamy calls after me as I speed up to make my way down the bricks.

I hold up my hand to quiet her and step off the path, so I'm walking along the edge of the greenery. I creep along the edge, peering through the leaves as much as I can to try to see movement. I get all the way to the edge of the sand before I see the man again. He's walking close to the greenery toward an outcropping of rocks, and I notice someone is walking in front of him.

"What in the living hell are you doing?" Bellamy hisses as she teeters on her impractical high heels and comes across the grass to me.

"Shhh," I shush her. "Look. See that guy?"

"You mean the fellow resort guest who probably spent a massive amount of money to be here peacefully enjoying the amenities of the island?" she asks.

"Last night when I couldn't sleep, I went out onto my balcony, and I saw him having what looked like a pretty intense conversation with Graciela."

"Graciela, the girl who takes care of your room?" she asks.

I nod. "When she came to my room this morning, I kind of teased her about it, but she was really quick to tell me it absolutely wasn't her. Socializing between guests and staff is strictly forbidden, and she is not about to lose her job, according to her."

"So, why are we stalking this guy?" Bellamy asks.

"Because I know it was her. They were right under my room. It wasn't hard to see her. And now there they are again," I say. "Don't you think that's odd?"

"That she's carrying on a secret relationship and doesn't want a stranger to know about it because it could get her canned? Not particularly."

I shake my head. "There's something strange about it."

The man has gotten far enough away for me to move closer. He reaches the rock outcropping and reaches in front of him to wrap his arms around Graciela's waist. Leading her around to the front of the rocks, he presses her back into them and leans down to kiss her. Just before he does, my mouth falls open.

"That's not Graciela."

CHAPTER FIFTEEN

"Are you sure?" Bellamy asks.

"Unless she grew several inches and dyed her hair in the last few hours, yes, I'm sure," I tell her. "That is definitely not Graciela."

The two move apart, and the man takes a step to start coming back in this direction. Bellamy and I move out onto the sand toward the water, so we don't look like we've been watching him.

"Maybe now you know what they were having such an intense conversation about," Bellamy points out. "Seems he's been socializing with more than one of the staff."

I glance over my shoulder and watch him walk up the edge of the greenery without the woman. She's still at the rocks, perched on top of one now, and looking out over the water.

"I don't know. There's something really strange about the way he's acting," I note.

"Why are you so fascinated by this?" she asks as we make our way back up the grass to where Eric is waiting.

"Because she's always fascinated by something," Eric offers. "She looks for mysteries to solve."

"I don't look for mysteries," I correct him. "I'm perfectly happy when there's absolutely nothing sinister or uncomfortable happening around me."

"You just saw someone kiss a girl by the ocean, and somehow you turned it sinister," Bellamy points out.

"I didn't turn the kiss sinister," I protest. "It's the whole situation."

"And by situation you mean the same man was having a conversation with one girl one night and kissing another girl the next day? And the girl he was talking to isn't spilling all the details of her personal life to you, a stranger who she kind of works for?" she asks.

"I don't know what to tell you. It's just sitting wrong."

"Maybe because snooping around after people for no good reason and finding drama where there isn't any doesn't fit on the island," Bellamy says.

Eric rolls his eyes.

"Oh, here we go talking about *'The Island'* again. She's turned it into its own entity."

Bellamy gives him a look that's meant to be scathing, but I see humor and affection in her eyes.

"I can't help it. Observation was trained into me my whole life. When I notice something that seems off, I latch onto it," I try to justify myself.

"The only thing off is that we are at a spectacular island resort on Windsor Island, and you are more interested in traipsing around after a man who is just acting like... well like a man, frankly. But, fortunately for you, you have your very own vacation coordinator right at your disposal. Let's go."

"Where are we going?" I ask her as she links her arm with mine and guides me up toward the path again.

"We're going to get changed into something active, and then we're going on a hike."

"You hike?" I raise an eyebrow.

"When I have a tropical paradise at my disposal, I hike."

* * * * *

Constance seemed thrilled to give us a full spiel about hiking around the island and offered us a map outlining some of the most popular trails. Following that map led us along to hours of weaving through the trees and flowers, high up onto hills. A note written on the side of the map promises us a spectacular surprise if we get to the end of the trail, and we've finally made it.

Stepping through the lush growth, we emerge onto a rocky cliff that juts out over the water. Bellamy gasps when she sees the incredible expanse of blue ocean in front of us. The sunlight sparkles on it, making the rolling waves look like they're bringing in glittering gold dust from the depths of some sunken treasure.

In the distance, I notice something fairly large bobbing near another rock outcropping. The longer I look at it, the bigger it gets.

"What are you looking at?" Eric asks.

"I think it's a boat," I say, nodding toward the shape. "It doesn't look like any of the ones available for rent."

"Maybe it's for supplies," Bellamy suggests. "They have to get food and things here somehow."

"That's true."

I walk out to the edge of the rocks to get a better look at the ocean. Peering down, I see the water coming onto shore. Rather than the soft glitter-flecked waves rolling in like those in the distance, these waves rise up to white peaks and smash to the sand. The curve of the rocks and the shadow of the cliff overhead makes the water look darker gray rather than the crystalline blue of the rest of the sea. It's suddenly harder to breathe, and for an instant, it feels like I'm toppling down toward the sand.

A hand in the middle of my back stops me, and I look up. Eric's eyebrows pull tight together over concerned eyes as he supports me with his hand.

"Emma, what is it?" he asks. "What's wrong?"

I shake my head, trying to get the thoughts out of it.

"Nothing," I tell him with a tense smile.

"I know you better than that," he says.

"It's not befitting of *'The Island'*," I tell him, trying to put some humor into my voice.

Bellamy steps up on the other side of me and shakes her head.

"That's fine. Tell us what's wrong," she says. "What did you see that's bothering you so much?"

I hesitate, not sure if I want to talk about it. But they're staring at me, and I know if I don't let it out, the thoughts will keep digging into me, so I gesture down over the edge of the cliff.

"I was looking at the water, and it made me think of Greg. Or actually his body. I just keep going back to him being found at the edge of the water. I know I've talked about it a thousand times and tried to figure it out over and over, but it just doesn't make sense to me. Greg didn't like the water. He especially didn't like the ocean. It seems so out of character to me that he would go through everything he did and be discharged from the hospital only to immediately go to a place he hated," I say.

"We've talked about that," Eric says.

"I know. I know we've said it's entirely possible him hating the water is why he went in the first place. It was a way to confront the fears and blocks he had in his mind from before he was captured. It was a way to grow his character and get a new lease on life. We talked about all of that, and it makes sense. Really, it does. For someone else. For anybody else. But I just don't see Greg doing it. Even after everything he went through. Even after the changes I could see in him while he was sitting in the hospital. I just honestly don't see that being the thing that comes to his mind. There are so many other things he could do that would challenge him and prove he could move forward with a new perspective. Going straight for the water doesn't make sense," I say.

"Especially that particular stretch of beach," Bellamy chimes in. "It was kind of a random area. That area didn't have any kind of special meaning for him, did it?"

"No," I say, shaking my head. "We never went there. I never heard of him going there. I never even heard him mention it. And even if we're going to go with the theory that he chose to go to the water for personal growth or to make a statement to the universe or something, that doesn't explain that blonde woman. The nurses said she didn't ever come up to the floor to visit him ever and wasn't there that day. All we see of her on the security camera footage is her leaving with Greg, and if you pay attention, he looks really happy to see her. Who was she? How did he know her?"

"And why hasn't she come forward?" Eric asks.

"Exactly. It's not like they were cuddling or holding hands, but the way they were acting with each other wasn't how people act when they first meet each other. Especially Greg. They knew each other. And that means she has seen the news about his death. It was splashed all over every channel for months. If she turned on a TV, looked at the internet, read a newspaper, or went on the Metro anytime in the last year, she knows he's dead. She saw herself in that footage that was shown over and over on the news. Yet she hasn't said a single word."

"Maybe she can't," Bellamy says. "There is the possibility that she and Greg left the hospital together, and whoever killed him did the same to her."

"Then why hasn't she been found?" I ask. "Greg was killed right out in the open. Not a single bit of effort made to conceal it or keep somebody from finding him. Why would the same person kill one person so publicly and hide another one, so she isn't found even a year later?"

"Unless they still have her," Eric suggests. "That is a possibility."

I nod. "It is. The problem is we don't know. It all comes back to the questions. It all comes back to not knowing, and that's the most infuriating part. If there was just one detail we could figure out. The smallest thing we could identify, we might be able to unravel the entire thing."

We stand in silence for a few seconds, staring down at the water, each lost in our own thoughts. Finally, I step back and shake my head. "Alright. That's it."

"What's it?" Bellamy asks.

"I'm done. That's all the thinking about that I'm going to do during this trip. I'm going to relax and enjoy being here," I tell them.

They grin at me, and Eric throws his arm around my shoulders, giving me a squeeze.

"Ready to start the trek back?" he asks.

"Absolutely." We start away from the edge of the cliff, and I look over at Bellamy. "Hey, vacation coordinator?"

"Yeah?"

"Next time you decide to bring us on a tropical survival march, think about packing a picnic."

Eric laughs and heads back down the trail at a jog.

By the time we get back to the hotel, we are hot and tired and agree to take a break in our rooms before getting back together in the evening. I say goodbye to them at the door to my room and head inside. Closing the bedroom door behind me, I go to the bed and pull my suitcase out from under it. I reach into the pocket on the outside and pull out a small box. Opening it, I run my fingers over the dog tags nestled inside.

CHAPTER SIXTEEN

TEN MONTHS AGO...

The first time Emma walked through the cemetery toward the grave that bore her mother's name, it was unsettling and upsetting. She didn't understand why the grave existed. From the time she was a little girl, not even twelve years old when her mother was murdered, she looked at the urn her father picked out and understood her mother's ashes were in there. During the dark and fitful times when she questioned everything, and the thought of a white sheet covering the stretcher made her wonder if she had really died at all, thinking about that urn forced her through. She could walk up to it and touch it, put her hands around it and see her mother's name etched into it. It wasn't the same as having seen her face, but it gave her something tangible.

It was like the urns that held her grandparents' ashes. They didn't give her any sense of who they were or the type of comfort they seemed to give her mother when she was alive. But Emma could look at them and understand that's where their bodies were. Not in Russia where they died. Not in a cemetery somewhere marked by a stone that blended in among the rolling landscape of identical markers.

They were there in those containers, and her mother was there in hers.

So why was she walking through a cemetery? Why did Bellamy find a death announcement that included information about a wake and a burial? It made no sense when her best friend went to Florida and found the information in the first place, and it made even less sense when she first crossed the grass and looked down at the stone with her mother's name on it.

She wasn't sure how she was supposed to feel in that moment. If it was supposed to be emotional in some way, or if it was supposed to bring her peace that she knew the body wasn't there. The problem was, she didn't know what to think. Anything could have been buried down in that grave.

But she didn't feel that way anymore. The sense of peace she felt might have been missing that first time but it came over her as she walked across the cemetery toward the plot. The May afternoon was bordering on hot, but the sunlight felt good beating down on her back. She got to the grave and knelt down in front of it. Brushing away some wayward bits of cut grass that clung to the stone, she set her mother's urn up against the stone.

"Happy Mother's Day, Mama," she whispered. "I thought it would be nice to come and visit you here today. But, of course, we both know you're not in there. So, I brought you."

Ian laughed beside her.

"I forgot how much like her you were," he said. "Maybe you weren't this much like her when you were younger. But you definitely have her sense of humor."

Emma looked at her father and smiled. That was the best compliment anyone could give her. She would cling to anything that connected her to her mother. Her long legs and blond hair were a hint, but being anything like her as a woman meant so much more.

Looking back at the grave, she reached over to the stone set close beside the one with her mother's name on it. There were a few more blades of grass covering the marker. She brushed them away, too.

"Hi, Elliot," she said. "This is the first time I'm seeing your gravestone. It looks nice. Better than that little white thing with a number on it, right?"

It still hurt her to think about how long he'd lain there in the potter's field, unidentified and without even the dignity of a real tombstone. She liked knowing he was here in the Florida graveyard now. Still watching over her mother, even after all these years.

Her father had given her all the information he had about the man she'd once known as Ron Murdock. According to him, Ron's real name was Elliot. He had no family. He started working with the rescue group Spice Enya years before Mariya even did but became particularly close to Ian and Mariya. They were the closest thing he had to a family when he was alive, and Emma wanted to be certain they remained his family even now.

He deserved recognition and respect. He spent years protecting her mother and facilitating the rescues of people in extreme danger. He put his life on the line countless times to ensure her safe passage from place to place and assignment to assignment. And in the end, he offered up his own life in one last effort to protect Emma.

She wished it hadn't turned out that way for him, but she also knew he didn't die in vain. It was because of him she started pulling the thread that eventually led her to understanding what happened to her mother. Emma could only hope that would be what he wanted.

She and her father sat at the graves with a picnic spread in front of them, talking and sharing memories, feeling truly connected as a family for the first time in so long. Mariya might not be there physically, but Emma could feel her. She could almost smell her and feel the touch of her soft cheek when she leaned down and kissed her.

They'd been sitting there for over an hour when a figure came across the cemetery toward them. The woman got to within only a few yards before she looked up, and Emma recognized her.

"Christina," she said, getting to her feet. "What are you doing here?"
"Hi, Emma," she smiled.

Her eyes moved over to Ian, and Emma noticed a fleeting expression of sadness mixed with happiness cross the woman's face. Christina Ebbots was the daughter of the head of the rescue organization, a man Emma now affectionately knew of as Grayson, a.k.a. Spice. Christina had provided vital clues to Emma throughout her journey, even if she didn't realize it at the time.

Once all the truth came to light, they discovered a connection. Like Emma, Christina had been kept in the dark throughout her childhood about the rescue organization and what it did. Her father had been a mystery to her, much like Emma's own parents. It wasn't until Spice died that she began to uncover everything her incredible father did.

"Mr. Griffin," she said. "It's good to see you."

Emma's father stood and walked up to the woman.

"Ian, please," he insisted. "I haven't seen you in so long. You were just a teenager."

Christina nodded.

"I'm sorry I never knew…"

Ian shook his head.

"That was the way it was meant to be," he told her. "From the beginning, we agreed not to involve you or Emma. It was too dangerous. You've done more for us than you will ever know."

Christina smiled and wiped away a single tear that slipped from her eye before turning to Emma.

"I hope you don't mind that I came here. I'm in Florida for a couple of months, checking on some of Dad's properties. Bellamy mentioned to me you were in town, and I kind of figured that you'd be here today," she said.

Even now that Jonah and Anson were arrested, Emma still felt uneasy about her whereabouts being publicly broadcasted. She'd long ago deleted social media and only kept a very tight-knit circle of acquaintances. Bellamy might be effusive and up-to-the-minute, but Emma was still hesitant, still on edge. She didn't know if she would ever feel completely at peace. Not as long as Leviathan existed in the world. But she had taken those men down, and she would do it again if she had to. Ever since the incident at the hospital, she'd taken it as her mantra: *'Let them come'.*

"Of course not," Emma said. "But is everything alright?"

"Yes. I found something that I think you might want to have. It's becoming clearer that my father was better at concealing things than I ever realized. Several of the properties he owned have hidden storage areas. I'm still uncovering more and going through them. Did you know about the hiding spot in the house you used to live in?" she asked, seeming to direct the question at Ian.

He shook his head.

"No," he said. "Where was it?"

"In the floorboards of one of the upstairs bedrooms," Christina told him. "I actually found it last year when there was a leak, and I had to do some repairs. I didn't think anything of the papers and things I found in there, but with everything that's been going on, I started going through everything again, and I remembered a specific envelope I'd seen. It fascinated me, and I didn't know what to think of it, but I think you'll understand, Emma."

"Alright," Emma said.

Christina handed her a thick manila envelope. Inside it was a set of car keys, an old cell phone, and a stack of papers.

"What is it?" Ian asked.

"When I found Elliot on the porch of the cabin where I was staying in Feathered Nest, he had no cell phone, no identification, no car keys. Nobody knew where he came from or where he was shot initially," Emma explained.

"That's right. You said he didn't have his dog tags," Ian said.

"No. And they weren't found near the porch or anywhere. But I think I know where they are."

Emma met her father's eyes, and he gave a slight nod.

Two days later, Emma's hand shook as she perched on a table in the upper floor hallway of Mirna's hotel near Feathered Nest, where the man known as Ron Murdock had made his very final public appearance. Her father and Mirna stood nearby, watching silently as she opened the vent on the wall. Emma's breath caught in her throat as she reached inside, and her hand touched something hard and cold. She withdrew it and looked down at the dog tags resting in her palm.

Mirna gasped.

"I have an appointment to have the vents cleaned next month," she said. "They only need to be cleaned and disinfected every few years. How could he have known they would stay there?"

Emma shook her head, still staring at the tags.

"He didn't," she said. "He could only hope."

Later she sat with the tags resting on her thigh, her fingers idly rubbing the dark red gem that indicated that he was assigned to protect Mariya. She opened the cell phone and read through the final message ever sent from Elliot, on the day he died. Just before getting out of the car in the woods behind cabin thirteen, he sent a text describing where he left his car, asking not to be identified, and where his tags could be found. His words were clear and unhalting. They carried no fear.

And someone had come behind him to gather his things.

Her father sat down beside her and handed her a cup of tea.

"He knew," Emma said. "When he sent that message, he knew he was about to die. He didn't want his car found or his tags advertised. He didn't want anyone claiming him."

"Because he wanted to protect you," Ian said. "He wanted to keep you safe and for you to know the truth. He knew about Jonah. He found out what he did. Just like he always swore to, he died defending your mother."

CHAPTER SEVENTEEN

Now I'm awake early the next morning, but for the first time in a long time, I actually feel like I slept. Whether it's catharsis from talking about Greg or just sheer exhaustion, I don't really care. Either way, I have energy and a clear mind. I've already taken a shower by the time the menu slides under my door, and I take a glimpse at it while I braid my hair. Graciela comes to the door just as I'm about to walk out.

"You look chipper this morning," she says. "Did you sleep well?"

"I did," I tell her, but looking into her wide almond eyes makes my mood sink down just slightly. "I'm sorry if I was too personal with you about that guy."

She smiles at me and shakes her head.

"You weren't," she says. "Here, try the juice this morning. It's my favorite blend."

She pours me a glass of juice, and I take a sip. It's delicious, and I finish it before handing her the glass back.

"Thank you," I say. "I think I'm going to go take a swim before the pool is overrun by beautiful tourists."

Graciela laughs as I dramatically swing a towel over my shoulder and head out of the room. Her simple dismissal of my prying into her relationship makes me feel a little better. Maybe I misinterpreted what I saw off the balcony. It doesn't change that she lied about talking to the man, but it's possible the conversation was innocent, and she just didn't want it to be overblown out of fear of consequences from management. I'm not completely convinced, but I'm willing to put it aside for now.

The harsh hit of emotion that came from looking down at that water affected me more than I would have thought. Just like I told Bellamy and Eric as we were standing there on the cliff, I need to get it off my mind. At least for now. Being here on the island is a chance to disconnect from all of that and just enjoy the relaxation.

And that's exactly what I intend to do.

Walking out onto the brick path, I lower my sunglasses over my eyes and look around at morning coming up around the resort. I'm clearly not the first person awake. A woman jogs past me in meticulously matched workout clothes that coordinate right down to the streak of color across her shoes and the thick retro scrunchie around her ponytail. Ahead of me in the grass, a small group goes through a slow sequence of yoga poses. I look forward to swimming a few laps in the pool, then maybe venturing into the ocean later. I'm not sure if I can hope for Bellamy's agreeing to such a slow and leisurely day, but I'm willing to dig my heels in against whatever agenda she's put together for the day.

A wrenching scream tears through the serenity. What had felt like a gentle, slow watercolor of morning rips into sudden glaring speed. I'm running toward the sound before I realize what I'm doing, and by the time I get to the pool, the jogger is clutching the wooden post at the gate and sagging towards the ground. One hand covers her mouth, barely muffling sobs.

"What is it?" I ask, placing my hand on her back.

She shakes her head, curling down further against her thighs. Her scream has jostled more people, and several come toward me from the beach and down the path.

"You need to tell me what's going on. Are you hurt?" I ask.

She shakes her head again and manages to lift one trembling hand to point toward the pool. I run to it, and my feet skid to a stop at the edge, my towel sliding down my arm to the concrete. Forget Bellamy's agenda. Right along with any chance of relaxing.

The body floating in the pool will be taking precedence.

A few people rush up behind me into the pool area, and I turn sharply to them. Law enforcement instinct kicks in, and I stand my ground firmly, holding up my hands to stop them.

"Stay back," I bark. "You can't get any closer."

"What's going on?" a young man asks.

"I want to see," a woman around my age says behind him. "What happened? Is someone hurt?"

She takes a step, but I press my hand closer to her.

"I'm sorry, but you're going to need to stay behind the gate."

"Who the hell do you think you are?" another man shouts, shoving his chest toward me. "You can't tell me what to do."

"Emma Griffin, FBI. And yes, I can tell you what to do, and you're going to shut up and do it."

"Where's your badge?" he demands, his lips screwing up and his eyebrows lifting as if he thinks he's being incredibly smart.

He doesn't know the answer to that question is that my badge is in my luggage because I don't make it a habit of accessorizing all my outfits with it when I'm not on duty. He also doesn't know that technically, since we're on a private island in international waters, the FBI doesn't have jurisdiction here. But he doesn't need those details. Instead of offering them to him, I look down at myself, then back at him incredulously.

"It doesn't go with this suit," I tell him flatly. "Someone needs to go to the lobby and get resort security. Right now."

"Emma!" I hear Bellamy shout from the path. "What's going on?"

She and Eric push past the small cluster of people now blocking the gate.

"Let them through," I say. "They're law enforcement."

Bellamy looks at me strangely as she jogs across the concrete deck.

"Is that applicable right now?" she mutters.

"Unfortunately, yes," I say, tilting my head sideways toward the pool.

"What happened?" she asks.

We walk over to the edge of the pool and look down at the body floating across the surface. The water around her is tinted a light red from a visible wound in the side of her head. I can't see her face, but judging only by her body, I guess she's in her early twenties.

"Holy shit," Eric mutters.

"Yeah. I was coming out here to swim, and I heard screaming. The woman in the teal workout gear was jogging and apparently came into the pool area and found her," I explain.

"Here," he says, shrugging out of the button-up shirt he's wearing over his swim trunks and handing it to me.

"Thank you," I say gratefully. "There's nothing quite like illegally taking over an investigation wildly outside your jurisdiction while in your bathing suit to put you in a good headspace first thing in the morning."

"You're not taking it over illegally," Bellamy offers. "You're... giving the professional courtesy of identifying and offering a guiding hand during an emergency."

"Remember that for my trial."

"What's going on here?"

We turn around and see a large, heavyset man in a dark navy suit coming toward us. Behind him is Alonso, as well as a woman I don't recognize.

"Are you resort security?" I ask.

"Yes," he nods, his Jamaican accent heavy.

Alonso steps up beside him, his usual serenely smiling face tight with worry and his hands wringing.

"This is Damion Campbell. Head of resort security. What's going on, Miss Griffin?"

"I don't know the specifics yet," I tell him. "I only just came on the scene a few minutes ago."

I step out of the way to reveal the body, and Alonso stumbles back a step. The woman standing with him tries to step forward, but he holds her back.

"This is Catherine Tovar. She's another manager of the resort," he explains.

"Hello," I say. I look to Desmond again. "I think it would be wise if you block off the area. I've seen several people go around the building, and I'm afraid they will be coming into the pool area soon. This probably isn't something you want them to see first thing in the morning."

Alonso nods almost too enthusiastically, making his head look like it's flopping rather than nodding.

"Yes," he says, gesturing toward the perimeter of the pool area. "We need to control access to the area. This is not an image I want plastered all over social media and associated with the resort."

"I see he has his priorities in line," Eric mutters to me.

"Do you know who it is?" Alonso asks before I can respond.

"No," I tell him. "We didn't disturb the body."

"Ma'am, thank you much for what you've done so far, but you should go with the other guests and leave the area," he says, reaching to put a hand behind my back so he can guide me away. "Please don't allow this unfortunate accident to ruin your stay with us."

"Has anyone called the police?" I ask, resisting him moving me.

"The island has no police force. We only have security. We'll call into the mainland for them to send someone out here," Alonso answers.

"How long will that take?" I ask.

"It may take some time."

He's still talking, but I realize Desmond has walked away and is at the edge of the pool behind us, using the end of a pool net to pull the body closer. I stalk toward him.

"What do you think you're doing?" I demand.

"We need to identify the body," he says.

"Without taking pictures of the scene? Making notes? Anything at all? You're just going to skim her off the water like a bug?"

"I'm sure he means no disrespect," Catherine pipes up, in a voice that should belong to a kindergarten teacher. "This is obviously a tragic accident."

"How is that obvious?" I ask.

She gestures toward the water, stammering slightly like she can't find the words.

"She's in a bathing suit," Alonso points out. "It looks like she came out here for her morning swim, slipped, and hit her head. That knocked her out, she fell into the water and drowned. It's horrible. She deserves the dignity of not being left in the water in front of prying eyes."

"The scene needs to be documented," I tell him.

Bellamy comes up beside me and rests her hand on my shoulder.

"I got a few pictures. Eric will help them get her out of the water and lay her down where she can be covered," she says gently.

"Thank you," Desmond says.

The flippant note isn't lost on Bellamy. She turns, flashing eyes to him.

"And as soon as that is done, I suggest you keep Emma right here with you until the police come, and you listen to every word she has to say."

"And why would I do that?" he asks.

My eyes lock onto his, daring him to use that tone again. I drop my voice low.

"Look me up."

CHAPTER EIGHTEEN

Taking off Eric's shirt, I ease myself down into the water with him. It's cold as it rises up my thighs and to my waist. We approach the body slowly. Behind us, Alonso, Desmond, and Catherine watch tensely. After taking my suggestion, they are more willing to step back and let us manage the situation until the police arrive from the mainland. I'm glad they aren't fighting me on it anymore. After seeing how they're willing to treat the situation, I am not about to leave this in their hands.

Eric positions himself on the opposite side of the young woman's body. I carefully tuck my hands beneath her to roll her over into his arms. Her skin is cold to the touch, and I take note of the stiffness of her extremities. As she turns onto her back, her long hair falls away from her face. The blood and water altered the color of her hair, making it harder to recognize, but now I know I've seen her face. It makes my chest clench.

"This is the girl from the beach yesterday," I tell Eric quietly. "The one Bellamy and I were watching."

I keep my hands under her body for more support as we carry her to the steps leading out of the pool. Desmond is doing what he can to keep gawkers away from the pool area, but he can't cover the entire perimeter, and I notice the clicking sound of several pictures being taken. It disgusts me, but all I can do right now is block as much of her as I can until we can get her covered. Eric and I carry her to an area off to the side of the deck, where a white trellis creates a partial enclosure to keep chairs and other pool supplies out of view of guests. I take a tarp from the top of a stack of chairs and spread it out on the ground to place her on.

Bellamy comes with a towel to place over her, and I stalk out to Desmond.

"You need to get every single one of these phones and delete the pictures," I tell him.

"Miss Griffin," Alonso starts, trying to give me one of his charming smiles. "We can't demand the guest's hand over their personal devices. There's no need to be disruptive."

"I don't know about you, but I find death a tad disruptive," I tell him. "There is a girl lying over there dead. Ten minutes ago, you didn't want anyone to have pictures of her in the pool because you didn't want it to show up on social media and make the resort look bad. Well, I can tell you that getting sued by her family because they found out about her death through a despicable picture being posted is going to look much worse for you. While he does that, you need to come identify the body."

"You want me to get close to it?" he asks.

"She is a human being," I snap. "You might want to remember that when her family comes to claim her and collect her things."

"Excuse me?" he asks as I start back toward where the body lies. I pause and turn to look at him. "Why would they come here to collect her things?"

"I saw her yesterday wearing a resort uniform. She's a member of your staff."

His face goes pale, but I don't have it in me to play nursemaid to him right now. My priority needs to be the woman dead in her neon purple bikini and finding out what happened to her.

Desmond has joined Eric and Bellamy at the body and is staring down at her when I walk back into the trellis area. I crouch down beside her and peel back the towel again.

"What are your first impressions?" he asks.

I glance up at him in a bit of a surprise but decide not to say anything about his sudden change of tune.

"She's been gone for several hours. When we were carrying her out of the water, I could tell rigor mortis has begun to affect the lower part of her body. That effect doesn't begin to set in until four to six hours after death and begins before the upper part of the body, usually in the eyelids and face. The injury on her head is perimortem. It happened before she died. There's indication of blood flow, which happens when a person is alive when an injury happens," I explain.

"What about her hands?" he asks. "Look at her wrist. How could her hand be bent like that if it takes hours for the body to stiffen up?"

I nod. "I noticed that, too. One of her hands is completely normal, but the other…"

"It looks like she's holding something," Bellamy points out.

"I'm not a medical examiner, so I can't make any real conclusions. But there is a phenomenon that can create that effect. Some doctors debate if it even exists, but it seems to have been documented in many instances. It's called cadaveric spasm. Essentially it means the moment death occurs; there is instant stiffness separate from and more intense than rigor. It can happen in the entire body or in only one area. Think about the victims in Pompeii. There are preserved bodies that show people crawling and reaching out, trying to survive. They died in that moment, and their bodies locked in that position, which allowed the mud and ash to solidify around them to create those casts."

Carefully lifting the bent hand, I examine it and notice something under her fingernails. The brown substance is deep under the middle two fingernails and shallower in the others. I can't tell what it is, but I don't disturb it so it can be collected later.

"So, she was trying to pull herself out of the pool when she died," Desmond concludes.

"Oh my god." I look up and see Alonso standing right at the

entrance to the enclosure, his eyes locked on the woman's face. "It's Rosa."

"Rosa?" I ask.

His eyes don't move away from her for a second, then he glances over at me, nodding.

"Yes. She's been working here for several months. I can't believe she's gone. How could this happen? She never had a problem in the water."

He goes back to staring at her, and I get to my feet.

"Have you called the police?" I ask. "Did you make sure they know the coroner needs to come?"

"Yes," he answers. "They're on their way."

"Good. Until they get here, we need to keep everybody away from the pool area."

"Absolutely," Alonso agrees with a nod. "I would prefer no guests to be around when the crew is working, anyway."

"Crew?" I ask. "What do you mean?"

"We can't expect the guests to swim in the pool without it being thoroughly cleaned. The crew will need to drain it completely. Proper cleaning and treatment will take time, so it's important to get started immediately."

I shake my head.

"No," I tell him. "Everything needs to be kept as it is until the police arrive. The other guests swimming should be your last priority right now."

"The expectations and needs of my guests are always my top priority," he tells me.

There's a hint of a threat in his voice.

"If you want to make this go smoothly, you will listen to me. There isn't a return policy on your staff. The police aren't just going to come, slip her into a bag, and go on their way like it's no big deal. They will want to know what happened, and if they show up here and there are a bunch of people scrubbing the scene clean, it will set off alarm bells."

"It was an accident," Alonso insists.

"Then it will be easy."

CHAPTER NINETEEN

"Emma, it was an accident."

There are those words again. It's Bellamy saying them to me this time, but they don't mean any more to me than when they came from the sleek, polished manager. I shake my head, pacing back and forth across her room. The police dismissed us from the scene an hour ago, and we came straight here. Within just a few minutes of us getting back inside, room service arrived with trays of food for us. It feels like a subtle form of damage control from the resort.

I'm sorry you saw a corpse floating in the pool, I hope these crepes provide you comfort.

"There's something else going on," I tell her. "That wasn't just an accident."

"Why not?" Eric asks. "Even the police investigators agreed with the initial explanation. Rosa went out to the pool for a swim, slipped, hit her head, and ended up drowning. It's awful, but it's not unheard of."

"Maybe," I admit. "But it still doesn't feel right. I just can't see that girl dying that way. You heard what Alonso told them. Rosa swam every morning. Every morning she went out to that same pool. You're going to tell me that all of a sudden, she ends up dying in a freak accident in the pool she swims in every single day?"

"That's what makes it an accident," Bellamy says. "You can do the same thing over and over, but that doesn't stop things from going wrong. Anybody can slip, especially if it's actually somewhere near water."

"No," I insist. "I walked up there on that deck. You did, too. It wasn't slippery at all. A resort like this makes sure their pool deck isn't slippery. People throwing down this kind of money to stay at a resort aren't going to want to end up on their asses in front of everybody when they're showing off their new bathing suit. And that's another thing. Did you see what she was wearing?"

"A... bathing suit," Eric says, drawing out the words because he doesn't understand their significance.

"A really sexy bathing suit," Bellamy adds.

"Exactly. That's not the kind of bathing suit somebody wears to do a few laps around the pool at dawn. That's a bathing suit meant to be seen by someone else."

Bellamy looks like she's thinking about this for a fraction of a second, then shakes her head again.

"Not necessarily. You can't judge what happened based on what she was wearing. Maybe that is the type of suit she wore every morning to do her laps because it made her feel good about herself, and she wanted to start her day off well. Or, from a less perky perspective, maybe it was a suit she didn't like the way she looked in, so she wore it as her motivation to work out harder every day."

"No. She was in full makeup. Her hair had styling product in it."

"For all you know, maybe that's just what she did. There's an agent in the fraud division named Jojo. She's a perfectly nice-looking woman. Clean, put together, obviously takes care of herself. She was out sick with the flu for almost three weeks last year. So I went to her place to bring her some soup. She opened the door in pajamas, slippers, a grimy bathrobe, and a full face of makeup. Far more makeup than she ever wore to the office. She told me she has always made it a point to wear makeup on her sick days because it makes her feel better. She's been doing it since she was in middle school, and her mother got her mascara for the first time."

"That seems like a lot of extra effort she's putting herself through when she's already sick. The last time I had the flu, I had to build up the energy just to roll over in bed. No way I could go through all that to put on makeup. And even worse... wash it off," I say.

"And that's fine, too. The point is, people wear makeup for all sorts of reasons. Jojo's makeup didn't mean she wasn't sick, and Rosa's bathing suit didn't mean she wasn't swimming alone."

"I know that. But it doesn't mean she was, either. It's something to think about. If she was planning on meeting up with someone for an early morning swim or was already with someone, even if it was an accident, that someone isn't saying anything," I say.

"That's a lot of vague terms for one sentence," she replies.

"And yet you know exactly what I'm saying. Somebody knows *something*. Somebody either saw her last night or this morning or was planning on seeing her this morning. And yet they haven't said anything to the police or anybody else. What is it that they're not saying? What do they know?"

"Maybe they don't know anything. Even if she was supposed to meet somebody this morning, either they were already gone by the time she went into that water, or they were late and with all the craziness going on around finding her body, didn't want to get involved," she theorizes. "Especially if it was the guy we saw her with. We already know she isn't supposed to be hooking up with guests. I'm sure she told him that by now, too. He's not going to volunteer that information."

"Why not? It's not like Alonso can do anything to her now."

"Be honest, Emma. Don't think just about her death. Think about the entire situation. Try to see it from his perspective. If you were in a secretive relationship you knew probably wasn't going to last more than a handful of days anyway and the person you were in a relationship with ended up dying in an accident, would you want to rush forward and put everything out there? Alonso might not be able to do anything to Rosa, but that doesn't stop the awkwardness or embarrassment."

"Embarrassed for having a relationship? Even if it was against the policies of Rosa's job, they are both adults."

"What if Graciela was lying to you and he actually was seeing both of them. Or maybe more," Eric points out. "Airing your dirty laundry is one thing. Dumping out the whole hamper and stringing up all the panties is another."

"If you don't want to think of it that way, how about this angle. If he admits he was with her this morning or that he was supposed to be, the police might take more interest in that crack in her skull," Bellamy says.

I stop pacing and look at her, leaning with my hands clamped on the back of a chair.

"That's another thing. The head injury."

"What about it?" Eric asks, nibbling his way through what seems like his fifth croissant. "You've seen this exact thing before. Unfortunately, it's not all that uncommon. People don't pay attention when they are out by the pool. They run or don't notice water on the edge. They lean down to scoop things out of the water and lose their balance. It doesn't take much to slip and hit their head. If they end up rolling into the water after, it can turn bad fast."

"You're right. I have seen it before. Which is why it's standing out to me. The injury on Rosa's head didn't look right to me."

Something occurs to me. "B, did you delete those pictures you took after you sent them to the police?"

"No," she says. "Thanks for reminding me."

"Before you do, let me see them."

She pulls the images up on her phone and hands it to me. I scroll through until the one she took zooming in on the wound in the side of Rosa's head. Flipping the phone back around, I show it to them.

"Look where that wound is. That's what was bothering me. When people slip and fall at the edge of a pool, they hit the back of their heads. It starts bleeding instantly, and then the person slides or rolls into the water. Rosa's injury is too far up the side of her head. How would she hit that place on her head if she just accidentally fell?"

I scroll back through the images to a wider shot of the pool, then sweep my fingers across the screen to tighten the image in on the edge. "And there's no blood on the edge of the pool. Nothing that shows where she supposedly hit her head and fell into the water so helpless and out of it she drowned."

"So, what are you saying?" Bellamy asks.

"Something happened to Rosa. Obviously. I just don't believe it was an accident. I need to find out who is responsible," I answer.

"No," Bellamy frowns. "You can't turn this into an investigation. That girl's death is sad. It was horrible and brutal. But it was also an unfortunate accident."

"I don't think it was," I argue, handing her the phone.

"Look, Emma, I agree. This is a bit suspect. And you're right about the blood," Eric starts.

"Thank you."

"But still. Even if there was foul play here— and I'm not saying there was— there is absolutely nothing we can do about it. As Bureau agents, we can't just pop in on random cases outside U.S. jurisdiction. We have to let local law enforcement handle this."

"So we just sit here and go back to our beach vacation, ignoring this poor woman? What about finding out the truth? What about justice?"

"I'm not saying that. I'm just saying that you're looking for a way to get involved," Eric says. "You're in a holding pattern, and you can't stand it."

"That's not what this is," I fire back angrily. "But you don't have to worry about compromising your career. I'm not asking you to be involved."

Storming past them out of the room, I stalk down the hallway toward mine.

CHAPTER TWENTY

I throw open the door to my room and am surprised to see Graciela inside. She forces a smile as she brushes tears away from her cheeks.

"When you weren't here when I first got in, I thought maybe I was going to get a reprieve from being startled by you," she tries to joke.

"Are you alright?" I ask.

She finishes wiping the counter and heads over to the balcony door.

"Yes," she says firmly as she sprays the door with cleaner and watches the drips glide down the glass. "It's more shocking than anything, really."

"You didn't know Rosa?"

"I knew her," she says, pulling a cloth from the pocket of her apron to start buffing away the cleaner. "But not very well. We have opposite schedules, so we don't work together." She pauses. "Had. We only talked a couple of times. But it's still sad to have someone you knew die that way. I just don't understand how it could have happened."

"What do you think happened?" I ask.

Graciela glances at me over her shoulder.

"I heard it was an accident," she tells me. "That she fell beside the pool."

"Do you believe that?"

Her expression is confused and tight as she moves on to work on the vanity mirror.

"I'm not sure what you're asking me."

"Do you think it's possible she could really have accidentally fallen and drowned?"

Her mouth opens like she's going to answer, then closes again as she reconsiders her words.

"That's what the police say. They told me she was floating in the water and had a cut on her head. I can't imagine anything else that might result in what happened to her."

I nod, not wanting to lead her in any way.

"Somebody mentioned that she swam a lot. Do you know anything about that?"

"She swam every morning," Graciela says. "I usually saw her coming from the pool when I was heading into the building to start my early rounds." Sudden emotion comes to her face, and she glances away. "I can't believe I won't ever see that again."

"Does this change how you feel about working here?"

"Of course not. What happened to Rosa breaks my heart, but it was only an accident. Accidents can happen anywhere. This opportunity is still my dream. Just like I'm sure it was for her," she tells me.

I'm still not convinced, but I let the conversation drop. Graciela finishes and gives me a friendly smile as she leaves. I think about what she said, trying to process the words and see if I can find any other meaning in them.

If she really was carrying on some sort of relationship with the same man that Rosa was, not knowing her well could have one of two reactions. In some instances, feeling betrayed by a friend can make a reaction to a situation like this more volatile and lead to violence, while having the other person be a stranger can make her more of an abstract idea, leading to more anger toward the cheating partner.

On the other hand, not knowing the other person can take the humanity away from her and create room in a person's thoughts to turn her into anything they want her to be. Without real-world knowledge about their personality or character to go on, it can be easy to transform them into a villain and turn all anger and wrath on them.

But I can't see Graciela being involved. It's not just that she's trained and funny, or even the hope and optimism that glimmer in her eyes even as she talks about the horror of one of her fellow staff members dying so suddenly. Taking what friendship we might have out of it, thinking of her only from the perspective of an investigator, I don't see her committing a crime like this. Her denials of talking to the man are suspicious, but there was little emotion in the denials. She didn't get worked up or defensive. She just brushed it aside. And as we talked about Rosa's death, she didn't get agitated or start story planting.

That's what I call it when someone potentially involved in a crime starts weaving their narrative early in the investigation, even before any attention or suspicion falls on them. Most of the time, they unknowingly end up offering more information than is asked of them. Producing pristine stacks of receipts that show their movements across every second of a given period of time. They're the ones who make 9-1-1 calls that include spiels about what they were doing and what their partners were doing for the day before they get to the fact that they have just found them murdered. Who slip details about a victim's perceived wrongdoings into conversations to lead toward a sense of blame, or who offer up their own theories about what happened that totally steer the conversations away from anything that might suggest them.

Story planting is common and often damning. It's like the person launching a kite into the air with a long tail trailing along behind it. Investigators who catch the end of the tail might be whisked away into the image the person is creating and be distracted from reality. But the investigator could just as easily yank the kite back down to the ground. Making excuses before they're asked for one. Giving information that isn't needed. Offering explanations that aren't wanted. They are all things that very often bubble up in a person responsible for something and tend to shine a light on them rather than being a distraction.

I didn't get any of that out of Graciela. She simply said she didn't know Rosa very well and that she heard it was an accident. She could be an exceptional actress, but I don't see any real motivation. The strongest reactions I've gotten from her are when she talks about working at the resort and how much it means to her. It doesn't fit.

The whole thing still isn't sitting well with me.

Alonso was upset by finding out about the death, but he also seemed very prepared to move forward from it. He immediately went into crisis intervention mode. Rather than wanting to cooperate with the police or thinking about Rosa, his mind went to how we could possibly gloss it all over and make it disappear, so the other guests of the resort weren't disrupted.

It's an indication of a good manager, somebody who really does care about the resort where he works, and about ensuring a guest's positive experience. But it was also smooth. Almost methodical, like this wasn't the first time he had to depend on those protocols.

Grabbing my computer, I bring it outside onto the balcony and pull up a search. It doesn't take much digging to find the information I want. More accidents at the resort.

The Windsor Palms Resort has only been open for a few years, according to everybody who's told me about it. Yet it's racked up quite an impressive list of incidents and unfortunate events. I go back into the room and get my notebook and pen to take notes of the reports.

Fell on the rocks by the water. Minor head injury.

Fell on the rocks by the water. Broken arm.

Fell on the rocks by the water. Death.

Fell down the stairs.

Burned in the kitchen.

Fell outside the lobby, cuts and bruises on her face.

Accidental prescription medication overdose.

Alcohol poisoning.

Several near-drownings.

Drowned in the ocean.

I bring my computer back inside, change out of my bathing suit into shorts and a t-shirt, and head out of the room. A couple is getting a bit too familiar with each other right outside the elevators. I'm in no mood to stand by and watch, so I take a detour around the corner to the staircase. This is definitely the kind of place where the stairs are only used for emergencies, but there's no alarm linked to it, so I head through.

I hear the muffled voices below too late to catch the door and keep it from shutting hard. The sound of the door echoes through the stairwell, and one of the voices hushes the other one.

"I have to go," the other voice whispers.

It's familiar. I move toward the bend in the flight of stairs to see if I can see anything.

"You need to listen to me," the first voice hisses.

There's no response, just the sound of footsteps and another door closing. I hurry down the stairs to the bottom floor, stepping out into the heavy air and darkening clouds of an oncoming storm just in time to see Graciela scurrying away down the path. And the mysterious man walking head-down in the other direction.

CHAPTER TWENTY-ONE

I want to chase after her to confront her about talking to the man again, but I don't. She's working, and if I keep pushing her, she's going to withdraw from me, so she doesn't put her job at risk. Besides, there's somewhere else I need to go. The list I made from the computer in hand, I head quickly toward the lobby. It has me trailing Graciela, but I stay far enough back that she won't notice me. Soon she veers off and heads down a narrow access path with a small sign marked for staff only. I continue past it and make my way into the main building and to the reception desk.

Constance looks up at me from the computer and gives me her practiced, professional smile.

"Good afternoon, Miss Griffin. Is there something I can do for you?" she asks.

It comes out of her mouth easily and unfettered; the words distancing her far from the events of the morning.

"Is there a manager available I can speak with for a moment?" I ask.

Her eyebrows knit together in a troubled expression.

"Is something wrong?" she asks. "Something I could help you with?"

I shake my head and give her a smile to put her at ease, realizing the request threatens her carefully balanced control over the resort and the experience of the guests.

"I just have a couple of questions I want to ask. I found a couple of things about the resort, and I just wanted to confirm them," I tell her.

She nods, still not looking completely convinced.

"Alonso is... occupied right now," she tells me, trying not to reference the continued efforts to put the resort back to normal when it is anything but. "I can call Catherine for you."

I smile at her again.

"That would be fine," I confirm.

She makes the call seamlessly, not giving away any emotion or concern in her voice as she tells Catherine a guest has requested to speak with her. When she hangs up the phone, Constance looks to either side, her eyes cutting through the lobby and taking note of everyone around before leaning slightly toward me.

"Is it true?" she asks. "Are you really... FBI?"

"Did someone tell you that?" I raise an eyebrow.

"It's all over the resort. People are talking about that girl's death, and they say you found her. That you're the one that took over the investigation."

I shake my head while trying to look as casual as I can.

"No," I tell her, "I didn't find her. I happened to be going to the pool when another guest found her. And, yes, I am a special agent. But it's not an investigation. You don't have to worry. There are certain protocols that need to be followed after there's a death, and since I happened to be there, I made sure they were put into place until the local police came. But I'm just a guest here."

She lets out a sigh, the sound seeming to release tension in her face so her mouth can curve up into a more genuine smile.

"Good," she says. "I wouldn't want you to come all this way only to get swept up into something awful."

"Not at all. The police did their investigation, and it was just a tragic accident," I reassure her, borrowing the words I've heard so many times that morning. "Everything I did is just for propriety's sake.

Red tape and all that. But, again," I hold up my hand like I'm making a declaration. "Just a guest."

"I'm glad to hear that," Constance says. "And I hope you are having a wonderful time."

"Absolutely. It's been incredible. In fact, I was wondering if there is any availability for next week."

Her eyebrows lift, and she goes back to her computer. A few clicks of her fingers across the keys seem to bring up the list of reservations coming up, and she scans them briefly before nodding.

"Yes," she says. "It looks like we have some spots available."

"Fantastic. It is even better here than I imagined, and I don't think a week is going to be enough for me." Reaching into my pocket, I take out my wallet and hand her my credit card. "Will you go ahead and put me down for another week? You can put this card on the reservation for when the covered trip runs out."

She's taking the card from me just as Catherine comes up to the desk. Dark hair swept up into a tight chignon on the back of her head defies humidity, and her minimal makeup enhances a serious yet warm face. She's one of those people who makes the thought go through your mind that she is pretty, but you can approach her easily. The perfect look for a woman who has the responsibility of a resort like this sitting on her shoulders.

"Miss Griffin, I wasn't expecting to see you. Constance, you should have told me it was her." Her eyes land on the card in the concierge's hand. "Is everything alright?"

"Yes," I tell her quickly before Constance feels the need to do any explaining. "I'm actually extending my trip. The island is so beautiful, and I'm so impressed by everything, I don't think I can get enough out of it in just one week. So, I decided to spoil myself a little."

Her eyes sparkle around the edges, and I know I've gotten the effect I want.

"That's wonderful to hear," she says. "But Constance said you wanted to speak to me."

"Yes," I nod. "Is there somewhere we can talk briefly?"

"Absolutely," she says. "As soon as Constance is finished with your reservation, we can step into one of the experience offices."

"I'm finished," Constance announces. "Thank you, Miss Griffin."

She hands my card back, and I slip it into my pocket. Catherine smiles and gestures for me to follow her. We cross further into the lobby and go down a hallway to a row of glass-enclosed offices that look out over the lush landscaping behind the building.

"These offices are set aside for our experienced team to help guests plan their dream trip. If there's ever anything you want to do or that you need during your stay here, you let us know, and we will introduce you to your own personal experience coordinator, who can handle all the arrangements for you," she explains.

"That's good to know. Thank you."

Rather than going to the desk near the floor-to-ceiling windows, Catherine sits in one of the plush teal chairs to the side.

"So," she starts, gesturing with one hand to invite me to take the other chair. "What is it that you wanted to ask about?"

"To be honest with you, I had never even heard of this resort until I won the trip here," I tell her as I sit down.

Catherine's smile is soft and amused.

"We pride ourselves on our exclusivity," she says. "Being the only destination on the island means we are in the unique position of creating a world for our guests that is separate and distinct from anything else. We want to be an oasis. There are many guests who return over and over because of the experience they have here."

"Oh, absolutely," I agree. "A few people have mentioned that to me. And I can see why. It's definitely a different world here. But that made me want to know more about it. I'm just that kind of person. One thing that I was particularly impressed by was how well Alonso handled the situation this morning."

Catherine's head lowers, and she shakes it slightly.

"So awful."

"Yes," I say. "And I know there was some tension initially, but the way he was able to stay in control and coordinate recovering the resort was amazing."

"He is very good at what he does."

"He is," I say with a smile. "Which got me thinking about it. That kind of calm and control usually doesn't just happen. It comes from experience. So, I looked into the resort, and I am curious about all the accidents."

Catherine's face falls slightly.

"The accidents?" she asks.

"Yes." I offer her the list I copied down from my research. "The resort hasn't been open for very long. But it seems like there have been quite a few serious incidents since it opened."

She scans the list.

"How did you find this?"

"Reports of incidents at tourist attractions have to be recorded if they require medical attention. Those reports are readily accessible if you know where to look for them."

Her expression recovers as she hands the list back to me.

"Then I'm sure you're aware that other resorts have similar accidents and incidents. It's just the nature of this type of destination. Water, natural environments, including rocks, and our alcoholic services. These attractions can pose risks if guests don't use them responsibly or behave improperly. I can assure you Windsor Palms is safe and will continue to be."

"That's all I needed to hear. Thank you."

She smiles, and we stand up. I shake the hand she offers me.

"If there's anything I can do for you or anything you need, please let me know."

"I will."

We walk out into the lobby, and she heads back to where she first appeared. I wait until she's out of sight to go to the desk again. Constance glances up at me.

"Was there something else, Miss Griffin?" she asks. "Is there any issue with the change in your reservation?"

"Oh, no," I tell her, shaking my head. "I'm already browsing online shops to find a wardrobe for my extra days. I just had kind of a strange question you might be able to help me with."

"Alright," she nods. "I will help if I can."

I glance around like I want to make sure no one else is listening and inch toward her, lowering my voice.

"It's actually about Bellamy and Eric, the two friends who are with me."

"Yes?"

"Can you be discreet?"

"Of course," she reassures me.

"Bellamy is concerned because the two of them… got caught up in the romance and beauty of the resort. If you're following me."

"I believe I am," she says with a slight nod.

"Good. Apparently, it happened on the grounds. She says no one saw her but is very worried there might have been security cameras hidden somewhere and now that footage exists. With the type of world we live in today, she is concerned it's going to end up in the wrong hands and follow her."

A knowing expression crosses Constance's face, and she nods, her eyes closing briefly before she looks at me again with a smile.

"I completely understand, ma'am. Don't worry; I won't let on to them or to anyone else. And you can reassure her that their secret is safe. The only security cameras in use at Windsor Palms Resort are the one covering the front door, one covering the service entrance gate so we can open it when deliveries arrive, and one that covers an area of the shoreline that is in the closest proximity to other islands, to ensure if someone from one of those islands accidentally comes here, we can guide them away."

"Oh? That's all the cameras?" I ask.

"Yes. There has never been an issue of security here, and we are confident there never will be. That is not a problem among our clientele. Of much greater importance is privacy." She tilts her head and gives a mischievous grin. "As your friend has proven."

I chuckle and step back from the desk.

"Perfect. That makes me feel better, and I'm sure it will make Bellamy feel much better."

"Anything else?"

"No. Thank you for your help," I tell her and walk away before she can give me the regular parting speech.

The twisting feeling in my stomach is tighter now. Talking with Catherine and Constance did give me the information I needed.

And cemented my belief that Rosa's death was far from an accident.

Something is happening at the resort, and I'm not willing to ignore it. I'm not looking for a murderer. But I won't turn my back when one finds me.

CHAPTER TWENTY-TWO

Rather than following the path back toward the guest rooms, I head deeper into the resort grounds. I haven't gotten far from the lobby when I see Alonso. He's already seen me, or I would do my best to avoid him. He waves as if to stop me and walks up to me quickly.

"Hi Miss Griffin," he starts. "I was on my way to stop by your room and check in on you to make sure you're doing all right."

"I'm fine," I tell him.

"Good. I do appreciate the help you gave this morning. Something like that is not what you expect to experience when you're on vacation," he says.

"I've seen far worse during many different times in my life," I shrug. "Besides, it was an accident. Seems something like that would be far more disturbing if her death had been intentional. But she fell. It's just a sad situation."

He stares at me for a few seconds longer than is really necessary but finally nods.

"It certainly is," he says.

He glances behind him as several young women come out of a small building with two of the attendants who helped carry the luggage when I checked in. There's another man in a suit very similar to Alonso's walking with them. He's younger and taller than Alonso.

"We are going down to the cabins now," the man says to Alonso.

Alonso reaches a hand out to him like he wants to touch his back and bring him closer to us.

"Frederick, I'd like you to meet Emma Griffin. She is one of our guests and the woman I told you about who was the first one to help this morning," he says. "Emma, this is Frederick Charles. He's the third manager at the resort, along with Catherine and myself. You haven't had a chance to meet him yet."

"Certainly my loss," Frederick says smoothly. "As you can see, I've been busy training the newest members of our staff family."

"It's nice to meet you," I tell him.

"The next rotation of leave begins tomorrow," Alonso says as if he's reminding the other man.

"Yes. Everything is ready," Frederick answers him.

"Excellent."

The group makes their way down the path in the opposite direction of the lobby. I hesitate, not wanting to be so obvious about falling into step right behind them, especially with Alonso looking right at me. He smiles at me as they get further down the path.

"What are the cabins?" I ask, remembering the conversation I heard pass between him and Rosa yesterday.

"The staff live in their own private village on the grounds. There are two dorm-style buildings as well as several individual cabins," he explains.

"It must be nice for them to be able to live right on the grounds. That saves them a fairly significant commute," I say.

He gives a short laugh.

"Yes. That would be a challenge for them to do every day."

"So, I'm assuming living in the village is a requirement for employment here? The staff isn't given the option to not live on the grounds if they don't want to?"

"It's considered a part of the compensation," he says, something in the way he says it telling me he's not thrilled about me asking these questions. "Our staff is very important to us, so we do what we can to show them their value through their compensation and the perks of their employment."

"It sounds like you do a good job," I say.

He gives me a teasing look.

"You aren't looking for a job, are you?" he asks.

I force myself to laugh.

"Oh, no. I'm happy where I am. Just curious. I have a couple of friends who have talked about getting out of the regular grind and finding a more exciting career. They might be perfect for something like this," I say.

"Well, we are always looking to expand our staff family with high quality, reliable members who are just as passionate as we are about giving our guests the most incredible experience possible. If you think they would be a good fit for that, feel free to give them my information."

"Great. Thank you," I say. "I'll do that."

"Do you have any plans for this afternoon?" he asks before I can start to walk away.

"I'm just exploring," I tell him, then point ahead to where the group went. "I haven't been on that side of the resort yet."

"There isn't anything in that direction but the staff village and a few buildings and lots used for running and sustaining the resort. Nothing for guest access."

"Oh," I say. "I was also considering renting one of the boats and going out into the water a little later."

"An excellent choice."

"What is out at the rock formation that juts out into the water?" I ask.

He narrows his eyes just slightly.

"I'm not sure what you're talking about?" he asks.

"Down past the building with the guest rooms, there are rocks that look like they go a pretty good distance out into the water. When my friends and I took a hike up to the cliffs the other day, I noticed a fairly large boat out there by the rocks. It looked like it was just sitting there, and I was wondering if there was some sort of tour or sailing I could sign up for."

"I'm not sure what you saw, but there is nothing like that offered at the resort. There are small watercrafts available for rent, and there is also the option of hiring someone to operate the craft for you for private tours and dinner cruises, but they are quite small. Nothing large enough for you to notice at that distance."

"Oh. It must have been a trick of the light," I shrug.

Alonso's smile returns.

"If you are open to suggestions, might I recommend a massage? It might help you relax. A technician can come right to your room for maximum privacy and indulgence."

"Thank you for the suggestion. I might just do that."

"Good." I start away, and he calls after me again. "Oh, and if you want a truly breathtaking experience, have Constance arrange for Joshua to give you his directions to the *Cascada Esmeralda.*"

"What's that?"

"The name means Emerald Falls. It is, pardon my pun, a hidden gem of the island. You might find a visit there enriching."

"Thank you again. I'll see if I can find a time."

"If you'll excuse me, I have guest requests to arrange. Please don't hesitate to let me know if there is anything I can do for you."

"Your suggestions are plenty. Thank you," I tell him.

He gives a nod that is almost a bow and starts toward the lobby. I stare down the path toward the staff village before reluctantly turning back around. Bellamy coming down the path toward me is a surprise, but she looks relieved when she notices me.

"There you are," she says.

"Was I supposed to be somewhere else?" I ask.

"No, I was just looking for you and haven't been able to find you. I wanted to say I'm sorry for earlier. Eric and I shouldn't have talked to you like that."

Walking past her, I shake my head.

"You're right. You shouldn't have," I tell her.

She falls into step alongside me.

"It's not that we think something is wrong with you or that you are making things up," she says.

"You're doing really well putting together this apology," I comment.

"We want you to be happy. We want you to relax and just get your mind off everything."

I stop and whip to the side to look at her so quickly she stumbles back a step.

"You don't think I wish I could just turn my brain off and not think about anything? You don't think that every day I just want to be happy and be able to relax? To not constantly have questions and theories and ideas running around in my thoughts? That's not what this is about, B."

"Then what is it?"

I hesitate.

"Do you really want to know?"

"Yes. Obviously, something is really bothering you about this."

"Come on. I don't want to talk out here."

We hurry to my room, and Bellamy sits down, looking at me with expectation.

"You already know the issues I have with the way Rosa's body looked and how she ended up in the water. But that's not it. Remember when I went back to the room to get my sunglasses when we were on our way to the pool?"

"Yes."

"When I went into the building, I almost interrupted a conversation in the hallway. I immediately recognized one of the voices. It was Alonso. He called the woman he was talking to Rosa."

"He's a manager of the resort. He interacts with everybody who works here," she points out.

"Yes. But you have to admit; there's something about him. The way he talks to everybody. He's nice, but it seems slimy. Like it's not that he's purposely being nice to people. He's just following some sort of script. He's playing a part. And the way that he acted when we found Rosa's body and were waiting for the police. He wanted to just hurry up and get rid of it all. He seriously thought it was fine to drain the pool."

"Being creepy, tone-deaf, and insensitive don't necessarily mean something is wrong. He seemed genuinely surprised Rosa was floating around in that pool."

"Yes, he did. And I'm not saying he wasn't. But that's not it. I'm still focused on the conversation he was having with Rosa. He was telling her that a guest requested cabin three for that night, and she was to prepare it for him and make sure his expectations were satisfied."

"Cabin three?" Bellamy asks. "I didn't know the resort had cabins. I looked at the website because I was considering booking another trip here, and there were only guest rooms and suites listed."

"Right. There are no cabins for guest rental. The only cabins I've heard about are the ones in the staff village."

She looks at me quizzically. "He was telling her to get staff quarters prepared for a resort guest? I know they keep saying to let them know if there's anything that will make our stay better, but that seems like a very strange request. I mean, I guess people with this kind of money might not have ever seen anything but all the luxury and indulgence of the resort and be curious about the way the staff lives. But that still doesn't seem like something they would actually do."

"No, it doesn't. And I just talked to Alonso. He introduced me to the other manager while they were showing new staff around. He mentioned the staff village, and then when I said I was going to explore that area of the resort, he stopped me. It's for staff only," I tell her.

"So, what are you going to do?" Bellamy asks.

"He really didn't give me any option. I'm going down there tonight to check it out," I tell her.

"Of course you are."

CHAPTER TWENTY-THREE

"So, what are we going to do up until then?" Bellamy asks.

"Where is Eric?"

"A guy we met at the pool recommended he go to the spa. Apparently, they do hot shaves and the types of manicures and pedicures that are acceptable for men. I'm not exactly sure what that means, but Eric thought at least the hot shave sounded like a good idea, so that's where he's going to be spending the afternoon," she tells me.

"Good. That means he's distracted and less likely to start in on the guilt trip again. I would like to try to find out more about Rosa if we can. I was thinking we could speak with some of the other girls on staff. And maybe a couple of the attendants. I've noticed that there only seem to be women cleaning the rooms. The room service and bellhop services are men. Most likely the girls would know Rosa better. Not necessarily, but if she's going to socialize with anybody, it would probably be with women who have similar jobs to her. So, if you could talk to the woman who cleans your room, I'll talk to Graciela. We can find out how they came to work here, what they know about Rosa, and see if we can get any information out of them about anything that might be going on at the resort without letting on that's what we're trying to do," I tell her.

"There's actually a different woman taking care of my room today," Bellamy tells me.

"Really?"

"Yeah. She came this morning, and when I asked where Tracy was, she said that she's on leave and that she'll be back."

"When I was talking to Alonso earlier, he introduced me to the other manager, then he reminded Frederick that the next round of leave begins tomorrow," I explain. "I thought that sounded really strange."

"It does," she shrugs. "But maybe that's part of working here. You get a certain amount of time off every so often?"

"Maybe," I say. "Well, see if you can talk to the one standing in for her. Find out what you can, and we'll meet back up later to go down to the village."

Bellamy agrees and leaves. When she's gone, I call the number listed on the directory in my drawer to get in touch with the housekeeping services. I request extra towels and wait for Graciela to get there. When she does, she has a confused look on her face.

"Did I forget to bring you towels this morning?" she asks.

I shake my head. "No. You did. I just wanted a few extras."

She laughs softly like she doesn't really know what to think about the request but isn't going to question it.

"Well, here you go. Is there anything else?"

"I actually have a question," I say. "You were telling me about how you got this job and all the perks and everything. It seems really amazing and like it would appeal to a lot of people. How often do new girls come here to work?"

"I have only been here for a few months, but there have been new girls that have come every couple of weeks. It can get very busy, and management never wants any of us to be overworked or end up with too much to do and not be able to get it done to their standards," she explains.

"Makes sense," I say. "Do you know which room my friend Bellamy is staying in?"

"Yes," she nods. "It's at the other end of the hallway."

"Right," I say. "And you know Tracy, the woman who takes care of her room?"

"Sure, she is one of the newer girls. She started here about a week ago. Maybe a couple of days more than that."

"That recently?" I ask.

"Yes, why?" she asks.

"When you first started working here, when was the first time they gave you leave?"

"Leave?" she asks. "I haven't taken any leave. I get two days off every week, but that's it."

"Bellamy said that she was told Tracy is on leave right now," I tell her.

"I can't imagine why she would get leave after only working here for such a short time. Maybe she has a personal issue going on that she needed the time off?" she suggests.

"Possibly," I shrug. "But I overheard the manager Alonso earlier. And he mentioned to Frederick that another round of leave was beginning tomorrow, which sounds like it happens regularly."

Graciela thinks about this for a few seconds, then shakes her head.

"I don't know. Like I said, she was hired at a different time than me. Maybe that was something she requested or a perk she was offered and I wasn't," she tells me.

"I have one more question. And this one might sound completely ridiculous. Have guests ever been able to rent one of the staff cabins for a night? Or are they used for any type of guest activities?" I ask.

Graciela shakes her head firmly.

"Definitely not," she says. "That is one thing that is strongly emphasized during training. No guests are permitted in the staff village. Not for any reason. Most of us live in the dorm buildings, anyway. There are some who live in the cabins, but those tend to be the married couples who work here, the older employees, and the upper-level staff."

"So, you live in the dorm?" I ask.

"Yes."

I nod. "Do you know who lives in cabin three?"

Her eyes narrow, and she shifts her weight.

"Why are you asking all these questions? Is something going on?"

"No," I tell her. "I'm just curious."

"That probably comes with being in law enforcement, doesn't it?" she asks.

"I think it does," I confirm. "My parents always encouraged me to be curious and figure things out, and both of them had careers that had to do with criminals and helping people."

She told me about how her mother encouraged her and supported her dreams, so hearing me mention my parents and finding that similarity between the two of us seems to put her at ease.

"I don't know who lives in the specific cabins," she says. "Why cabin three?"

"I just thought I heard somebody talking about it," I tell her. "It must have been a mistake."

"Anything else?" she asks.

"No, thank you. I really appreciate you humoring me."

"No problem. Let me know if you need anything else," she says.

When she leaves, I take out my phone and text Bellamy that I'm going down to the lobby but will be back in my room soon. I make my way directly to Constance's desk.

"I was just talking with Alonso a little while ago, and I mentioned to him that I may know some friends who could possibly be interested in working here. He said if they are, to reach out to him, but I forgot to get his card. Do you happen to have one available?" I ask.

"Absolutely," she says. She reaches into a drawer in front of her and pulls out a card. "This is his hiring information. It's probably what he meant for you to have. Anyone who is interested can just follow this link and fill out the initial application from there."

"Oh, perfect," I say. "Thank you."

Tucking the card in my pocket, I start back to my room. Before I get all the way to the door, a figure steps out from around the side of the building and startles me.

"I'm sorry," a deep voice says, and when I turn to look at him fully, I realize it's the man I saw both Graciela and Rosa speaking with.

"You," I say.

"Is it true you're with the FBI?" he asks.

"I am a special agent, yes," I tell him. "But for now, I am mainly a consultant more than an active agent." I hold out my hand to his. "Emma Griffin."

Eric is right. The Bureau has no jurisdiction here, which means we have no real right to be involved in the investigation. We can't perform any arrests and we have no legal standing. Distancing myself from my role as an agent will not only put people at ease so they are more likely to cooperate but might lessen the negative press that might happen if this all explodes.

For now, I'll lean into being a consultant. It sounds official enough to earn trust, and distant enough to not make someone feel as if he is facing imminent arrest.

He doesn't take my hand but looks almost frantically from side to side and takes a step closer.

"Emmanuel Vargas," he says quickly, more like an appeasement than an introduction. "I need to speak with you."

"You were with Rosa before she died," I say. "And I saw you speaking with Graciela."

"I can't talk about it right now. I'll contact you tomorrow. It's extremely important."

I barely have a chance to nod my acknowledgement before he rushes away. As I head up to my room, I call Bellamy.

"Remember the mysterious man Graciela insists I didn't see her speaking to, and who hasn't made a statement or anything even though we saw him with Rosa, not a full day before she died?" I ask.

"Yeah," she replies.

"I just had a talk with the phantom."

CHAPTER TWENTY-FOUR

The sun has already started to set, and the temperature has dropped enough that my shorts aren't enough anymore. I head up to my room and change into jeans, then call for room service for dinner. I don't want to go down to the staff village too early, but I also don't want it to be so late that everyone is asleep. Part of the reason for going down there is to see how much activity I can witness and if it will tell me anything.

When I finish eating, I call Bellamy to ask if she's ready to go. She says she'll meet me downstairs, and I grab a light jacket to put on over my tank top before heading downstairs to meet her.

Unsurprisingly, Bellamy is already outside the building when I step out.

"Have you spoken to Eric?" she asks.

"No," I tell her. "Have you?"

"No," she shakes her head. "I sent him a couple of texts, but he hasn't responded since he left the spa."

"I'm sure he's fine. He probably got a deep tissue massage and ended up passing out when he got back to his room. You know how wound up he gets. He's like a rubber band. Really effective when it's tense, but as soon as you loosen it up, it's no good."

She laughs.

"That's true. Alright, so what's the plan? How are we going to do this?"

"We're going to walk down the path to the staff village," I tell her.

"That's it?" she asks. "We're just going to walk down there?"

"If we don't want to call a bunch of attention to ourselves, yes. If we have to come up with something else when we get there, that's what we'll do. But for the most part, the least complicated path is the best one to follow. And in this situation, the least complicated path is the brick one that leads right past the lobby and down to the village," I tell her.

She looks a little disappointed, but she doesn't argue, and we make our way down the path. As we go, I pay attention to the people around us. Like I did the first night, I notice couples walking around together, and in some places, small groups gather and head off to different areas of the resort.

For the first time, I notice a few of the faces look familiar. I recognize two of the housekeepers standing with one of the men who carried our luggage and another man I don't recognize. They have their heads close together and are talking quietly, then another man approaches, and the conversation ends. The women smile at him, and they walk away with the attendant close behind.

"Did you find out anything from the housekeeper?" I ask.

"There wasn't a lot to find out, honestly," Bellamy replies. "She told me she has always dreamed of traveling the world and seeing exciting new places. She grew up in some tiny little town in Texas and thought she was never going to get out of it, but when she heard about the opportunity to work here, it sounded incredible. They were offering good pay, benefits, and a ton of perks. They told her they would make sure her family was taken care of, offered her room and board, the whole thing."

"Just like Graciela," I reply. "That sounds exactly like what she told me."

"I'm guessing if you spoke to everybody on staff here, you'd find that story being told quite a bit. Working on an island resort isn't exactly the type of job people take lightly. They live here on the island without their families or friends, so it takes a type of person who really wants an adventure to accept a position like this," she says.

"Or someone who desperately needs the opportunity," I muse. "Did you ask her about taking leave? Did she say anything about when she got time off or for how long?"

"No." She shakes her head. "She told me she only just started working here a couple of days ago, so she hasn't heard anything about time off."

"She just started working here? So, she was probably in the group who was being shown around when I spoke with Alonso and Frederick earlier."

"I doubt it," Bellamy says. "You said they were being trained. She came by my room last night when I requested an extra pillow and then was back this morning. I don't think they would let somebody brand new work by herself before she even went through training."

"You're right," I say. "That doesn't make any sense. Of course, none of this does. Oh, I can't believe I didn't tell you this. I mentioned the boat that I saw to Alonso."

"What boat?" Bellamy asks.

"When we went on the cliff, and I pointed out that boat. I mentioned it to him, and he said he had no idea what I was talking about. There isn't anything like that at the resort, and he can't imagine why there would be anyone out near those rocks."

"That's interesting," she says.

"I thought so, too." We are well past the lobby at this point. Ahead of me, I see the brick path veer and a sign marked 'Staff Only' posted near the fork. I nod at it. "We're getting close. Remember, we're not supposed to be here, so we need to be discreet."

"This is so *Dirty Dancing*," Bellamy whispers. "Sneaking into the staff only area to see what we can find."

"Yeah," I mutter bitterly. "Nobody puts Baby in a corner, but somebody put Baby in the deep end."

She gives me the side-eye.

"Damn, Emma. You can't even give me ten seconds of Swayze fantasy?"

"You can have your fantasy when I know what happened to Rosa."

She turns to look at me more fully.

"You really believe she was murdered," she says.

"Do you think I would go through all this if I didn't? Graciela lied to me, and Emmanuel looked terrified when he talked to me. The second Alonso got over his shock, he all but told the police to wrap Rosa up and toss her out with the recycling as long as he could get the pool back open before it got too hot in the afternoon. This isn't normal, B. I know we're on vacation but put on your FBI hat for just a minute. Think about it logically. Something happened, maybe several things that people don't want anybody to know about."

"Which means you need to know."

"Someone needs to."

We continue down the path and slip past another staff only sign. A tall wooden fence rises up on either side of the path, blocking our view.

"The gate is open," Bellamy whispers.

A wooden gate hangs loose; the latch tucked back as if it's rarely locked into place.

"They're probably not very worried about this area being secure," I point out. "Most guests aren't going to be interested in going to the staff quarters. And if I'm right, the ones who do aren't going to get any resistance."

"The only question is, why do they want to?" Bellamy says.

"Exactly."

We exchange glances, confirming with each other we're going to keep going. This would be the moment when we could turn back. We could say we went to the staff village, which was our intention, to begin with. But that's not enough. Seeing it from afar doesn't tell me anything. I need to know what's in there that might have been enough to kill for.

Beyond the fence, the path forks and widens. The same trees and flower-studded vines that create the lush backdrop of the main grounds of the resort thrive here. Without the restrictions and tight control of the manicured landscaping, they are even more beautiful. The fragrance from the night-blooming flowers is almost dizzying and mesmerizing. It's too stunning here for the ugliness I worry is simmering just beneath the surface.

We move down the path to the right. We don't have to go far to see the dorm buildings ahead of us. We then turn and make our way down the other side of the fork until we see rows of small cabins built of dark wood and topped with curved tile roofs. A rustle of voices behind us sends a shock of energy up my spine. I grab onto Bellamy, pulling her into the trees.

From where we're crouched, we see two of the housekeepers scurrying up the path. They've changed out of their uniforms for the day but are each carrying a covered tray.

"Room service?" Bellamy whispers.

"I don't think that off-duty housekeepers are bringing room service to other employees," I tell her.

The women pass, and almost immediately after them follows the man who brought Eric's luggage to his room. It would be too loud for us to move through the growth to follow them, so we have to wait until they've passed before we can go back onto the path.

Staying close to the shadows under trees, we follow the few yards it takes for us to see one of the girls climb up onto the porch of a cabin. She takes a key from her pocket and turns it in the lock, then disappears inside. The other housekeeper repeats the process in the next cabin over while the man stands outside, positioned between the two, and stares.

A few minutes later, the first of the housekeepers come back out of the cabin. Her tray is now empty and hanging from her hand by her side. She walks up to the man and hands him a roll of cash. I glance over at Bellamy.

"Someone is paying a lot of money for whatever they have on those trays."

"Drugs?" she asks.

"I don't think it was a burger and fries."

CHAPTER TWENTY-FIVE

"Look," Bellamy hisses, grabbing my wrist and nodding toward one of the cabins.

Another of the attendants who helped us with our luggage steps out, along with another I recognize as walking with the group Frederick was showing around the resort. They are only paying attention to each other, talking closely and gesturing as they come down the short set of steps to the porch.

Hoping she will follow me without me having to say anything, I dart across the brick path and into the shadows between two of the other cabins. We press against the side of the building and inch around the back and into the space between the next two. This allows me to lean around and peer between the spots on the side of the porch to where the two men are.

I expected them to come down the path back in the direction where we walked up. Instead, they turn in the other direction. The housekeeper who came out of the cabin first walks behind them, none of them seeming to care that the other one never came out of the cabin she entered. They walk past the last two cabins visible along the path, then turn a corner that brings them deeper into the low-hanging trees.

I wait for a few seconds, then run back to the area behind the cabins. It's open without any fences or other barriers to divide the land into yards or private space. That makes it easy to run behind them, but it also means at any second someone could come out of one of the back doors and see us.

If it gets us any closer to getting our questions answered, the risk is worth it.

The row of cabins goes further than I thought it would. The size of the dorm building makes it look as if it could house quite a number of people, so I didn't think they would need many cabins. But as we continue along the row, we find more than a dozen more cabins dotted along the curved path. At the end of the row, the last cabin sits right up against the darkening rainforest growth.

Bellamy and I carefully move between the two cabins to go out onto the path, looking around to make sure no one notices we're there. With the apparent size of the staff, it's entirely possible anyone who did happen to see us wouldn't be able to immediately tell we didn't work there. But I don't want to take that chance.

The path is empty in front of us. Faint pools of light from small lights in the path illuminate our way. It gives us just enough visibility to see what's ahead of us and make our way down the path without tripping. But it's dark, and there are shadows, and the wind is moving in off the shore. I can smell the ocean air.

The path continues to curve around in a lazy oval until several yards ahead the trees open out, and I see the glint of the dorm building in the moonlight.

Bellamy and I step into the shadows again and ease closer. The two men and the woman aren't visible anymore, but when we get close to the end of the path, I see a large black van parked close to the side of the building. The back hatch is open, but there's no one near it.

"I want to see what's inside," I tell her.

"Emma, no. Someone is going to see you."

"Not if I move fast enough. And if they do, I'll just tell them I'm lost. They've believed everything else I've fed to them."

I take off toward the van and hear Bellamy mutter a profanity behind me before she runs to catch up with me. We get to the van and crouch down behind it, staying there for a few beats until we're confident no one has seen us. Moving around to the back, I peer around into the inside.

"Empty," I curse under my breath, then look at Bellamy. "No seats, nothing."

"A delivery?" Bellamy asks. "This late?"

I shake my head slowly, shrugging.

"I don't know."

A door on the side of the building opens. We scurry back behind the van before diving out of view into the shadows. I hear two men's voices.

"How many?"

"Five."

"That's too many. It will be noticed."

"No. I have that covered. It's what they want."

"What about the special request?" a woman's voice surprises me.

"Got it."

"Perfect."

"Come on," I whisper to Bellamy, tugging on her arm. "We need to get out of here."

We run down the path until we get to the cabins, and then follow the same route we took behind the buildings. I feel like I don't take a breath until we're beyond the wooden fence of the village and past the 'Staff Only' sign.

"What the hell is going on in there?" Bellamy asks.

"I'm not sure, but I don't think it's advertised in the resort brochure."

"Did you recognize the voices?"

"No," I shake my head. "The men who carried our luggage didn't say anything to me, so I don't know if that was them. I'm assuming it was, but I can't be sure. That woman's voice, though. I feel like I've heard it. She wasn't talking loudly enough for me to be sure, but it sounded almost familiar. Maybe one of the guests."

"Why would a resort guest be in there with them?" she asks.

"I don't know."

We walk in silence until we get back to the guest building.

"What are you doing now?" Bellamy asks.

"Going up to my room. I need to try to get all this straight in my head. I'll give you a call in the morning."

"Okay."

We part ways in the hall, and I head to my room. When I step inside, I notice a piece of folded paper on the floor, like it was slipped under the door. It's folded in half hastily, and the printing looks like one of the menus delivered every morning. But when I pick it up, I see writing inside.

'He didn't hire her. Room #502. Tomorrow. E.V.'

As soon as I read the note, I burst out of my room and rush to Bellamy's. Her eyes are wide when she answers my series of rapid-fire knocks.

"What's wrong?" she asked.

I push past her into her room and hold the note out to her.

"This was sitting on my floor when I got into my room," I tell her.

She reads the note, then lifts her eyes to me.

"E.V.?" she asks.

"Emmanuel Vargas," I explain. "The man we saw with Rosa and who I know I saw talking to Graciela."

"What does it mean he didn't hire her?" she asks.

I shake my head, starting to pace again.

"I don't know. But he's trying to tell me something."

"Are you going to wait until tomorrow to talk to him?" she asked.

"I don't want to. But if he is specifically saying to come tomorrow, there's a reason. We both saw him with Rosa, and now she's dead. I don't want to cause him any danger."

I pace for another few seconds. "Damn it. What does he mean? He didn't hire her. I'm assuming he's talking about Rosa, but who is 'he'?" A thought snaps into my mind. "Alonso told me if I knew anybody who might want to work here, to get in touch with him. Maybe he handles all the hiring?"

"It's possible," Bellamy nods.

"I have a feeling he's not going to tell me anything," I say. "But Constance might. She gave me his card when I asked for his contact information. Maybe she knows who handles all the hiring around here."

"I doubt she's still working this late," Bellamy says. "You'll have to wait until morning to talk to her."

"There has to be someone down there at the desk. Who else is going to take care of whatever the guests need?"

I can hear the bitterness in my own voice, and Bellamy lets out a breath. She knows she can't stop me.

The door opens before I can leave, and Eric comes in. His eyes widen in surprise when he sees me.

"Hey," he says. "I didn't expect to see you in here."

"Clearly," I say, my eyes are dropping down to the key in his hands. "Just coming by to check on Bellamy?"

They exchange glances, but neither of them offers any information. I decide not to push it. There isn't time to listen to them dance around whatever they're avoiding telling me. Eventually they'll tell me what's going on between them.

"How was your afternoon?" Bellamy interjects, quickly rerouting the conversation.

"Actually, it was a little strange," he says, coming further into the room.

His movement toward the small refrigerator to the side is familiar, and when he opens the door, I can't help but notice bottles of his favorite beer inside.

"What do you mean strange?" she asks.

Eric crosses the room and drops down onto one of the chairs in the seating area. He grabs a bottle opener from the table in front of him and cracks his bottle open.

"The guy I met at the bar, Luke, has been here a bunch of times. He acts like it's his own personal summer home. When he talked about it, he called it a spa, but that's not exactly what it was. When we got there, a guy brought us into a lounge area and gave us menus of the different services they offer. Facials, massages, hot shaves, that sort of thing. Luke told me he always gets a hot shave and a foot rub and likes to order a cigar to have during it. I figured it was vacation, so I'd go for it and told him I'd do the same thing. Then he asked if I wanted any kind of enhancement for my cigar."

"Enhancement?" I raise an eyebrow.

Eric takes a sip of his beer and nods.

"My same reaction. He said to tell them I was feeling tired and wanted to enjoy more of the resort's amenities, so I needed some energy. He wouldn't explain what he meant but just kept saying the resort makes sure every experience is the best it can be. We both got called back, and the woman who came in to do my foot rub asked if there was anything else I wanted. I asked about the enhancements, and she asked who recommended them. I told her Luke, and she asked if he told me what to ask for. I told her what he said about the energy, and she asked if he said anything else. I told her no, and she just offered me a couple of different types of cigars."

"That's it?" I ask.

Eric nods, and Bellamy looks at me questioningly.

"What's wrong with that?" she asks.

"Different brands of cigars are different in their flavor, but there aren't any designed to give you energy. They were offering Eric drugs."

CHAPTER TWENTY-SIX

"Then why didn't they say that?" Bellamy asks. "Why didn't they actually offer them to him?"

"Because he didn't say the right things?" I say. "She was probably looking for specific words. Eric didn't know whatever code to ask for. Probably helps them to keep a wall of plausible deniability. Only people who know the right thing to ask for are given whatever... 'enhancements' they have on offer."

"Everybody here knows Eric is in the FBI," Bellamy points out. "Why in the hell would somebody offer an FBI agent drugs?"

"Luke checked in after the body was found," Eric says. "He might not know. And if he does, it could be a test. Whoever is funneling the drugs into the resort could be testing the people working in the spa. They want to make sure that they are using the right words."

"That's a risky game," Bellamy notes.

"I don't think it was a game," Eric tells us. "If they were going to test the staff, they'd choose literally anyone else."

"Could Luke have something to do with the resort other than just being a frequent flier guest?" I ask.

"What are you thinking?" Eric asks.

"You say he checked in after the murder happened, so he wasn't around to hear you are FBI. But just because he wasn't here doesn't mean he wouldn't hear about it. You said he comes here all the time. That's something I heard from Constance up at the front desk, too. People come back here over and over because they love the atmosphere so much. There are probably several other guests here who have overlapped his stays. They're friends. You don't think as soon as he showed up, they wouldn't fill him in on a woman found floating around dead in the pool and a swarm of FBI agents swooping down? That's going to be the first thing he hears from the guys sprawled around the newly reopened pool. 'Here's a cocktail, did you hear about the dead chick?'"

"So, you think he knew who I was when he invited me?"

"I think he knew before he ever started talking to you."

"Why would he do that?" Bellamy asks.

"They're offering drugs to their guests to give a boost to their resort activities," I say. "Who better to have on their side than crooked law enforcement? They must have brought Luke in as a connection. He comes here enough that he knows the clientele, and he has sway over them."

"So, they use him like a saloon girl," Eric continues my thought process. "He pays attention to the guys at the resort and chooses ones he thinks are good for wanting to enhance their stays, hangs out with them, and then brings them to the lounge. He probably gets a cut of the cost or his own drugs free."

"But why didn't he give you the code words?" I ask. "I can't imagine you would be the first person he would do that for, so he knows what he's doing. Why would he let it drop like that?"

"Distracted?" Eric suggests. "It's been a while since he was here at the resort, so he was getting antsy to get in for his own foot rub and enhanced cigar?"

"Or he changed his mind. Something about the way you reacted told him you weren't the kind of guy they wanted around to help," I add.

I look down at my phone, and Bellamy gives me a questioning tilt of her head.

"What are you checking?" she asks.

"The time," I say. "There isn't anything on the hiking trails that says they close at a certain time, is there?"

"What are you up to?" she asks.

"I need to go back up to the cliff," I say. "I need to check something."

"It's really getting late," Eric says. "You shouldn't be walking around up there in the dark."

"I'll be fine," I tell him. "This can't wait until morning."

"Then I'm coming with you," he insists.

"No," I say. "If we're right about Luke considering you to be added into the drugs loop here, they already have eyes on you. You don't want to call more attention to yourself. All I'm going to do is walk up there and back. And I'm going to take a direct route, rather than the long twisted one Bellamy decided would be a good idea. It shouldn't take long."

She's pouting at me, but Bellamy looks relieved I'm not going to be adventuring around the islands all night.

"How about me?" she asks. "Do you want me to come?"

"No," I tell her. "The two of you need to stay here and be visible. Make sure people see you. Get dressed up and go have cocktails in the lobby or go for a stroll on the beach. Swim. Do something and make sure you talk to people. Maybe even request a couple of things from the desk or one of the managers. Make it obvious that you are just having fun and enjoying the resort."

"Why would we do that?" Eric asks.

"Because what kind of best friends would allow someone to go creeping around on barely tamed island hiking trails by herself at night?" I ask.

"That's not reassuring, Emma," Bellamy calls after me as I head to the door. "You're not making me feel better."

The door closes behind me, and I rush for my room before she can come out and argue with me. Grabbing the small day pack I brought with me, I toss a few supplies inside and leave. Just like it has been the last few nights, the resort is alive in the fragrant night air. Couples milling around, men making their way out to the lobby, women on the prowl going to the pool or the beach to try to make a catch before bed. A few glance my way, and I make it a point to smile at them, giving them a full view of my face and exchanging a couple of words when I can.

I'm planting seeds, dropping breadcrumbs. People will know where I am and when.

The path Bellamy took us on the other day was winding and complicated, giving us a meandering tour of a large section of the island. I go for a more direct route. It's still not a fast or easy trek, but it cuts the transit time down to a more manageable forty minutes, and I'm not as tired when I get to the top of the cliff. There is still a disconcerting twinge in my lower back that reminds me I need to get back to my jogging and maybe take my seasonal clothes off the workout machines where I hung them in my house.

I make my way to the edge of the rocks and look out over the water. The waves look like tiny slivers of silver and black, reflecting off dueling patterns of starlight and shadow. But the moon is nowhere to be found. The clouds have come in, and the moon only shows its face in short, quick flashes before peeking back under the cover of darkness.

I doubt the flashlight on my phone I used to help me get here is going to do much good, so all I can do is get closer and try to see what might be ahead of me. Everything is still too dark, and I look around to find an alternative. There's another outcropping of rocks to one side. It's not as high as the one where I'm standing, but it seems to push out further into the ocean. I get back on the path and orient myself, trying to figure out how to get to that spot without instructions.

It takes some trial and error, but eventually, I climb up a steep edge onto the top of the cliff. I'm slightly lower, but the angle takes advantage of the sliver of moonlight glowing under the storm clouds, and I'm able to get a glimpse of the spot I was trying to see across the water. The dark rocks jutting out far into the ocean look even more ominous, but it's the shape of the boat that catches my attention. It sits right where I saw it the first time, close to the rocks and not moving.

A sudden blast of lightning illuminates the angry waves washing up on the sides of the boat and the empty deck. With it comes a sheet of cold, soaking rain. Muttering under my breath, I walk away from the edge of the cliffs and start back down the path. The rain comes harder, and the forest around me gets dark to the point that I can't see further than a couple of feet in front of me. My eyes sting from the tiny, hard drops hitting them at a harsh angle, forcing me to look down. It makes it even harder to navigate where I am and what I'm doing.

It doesn't take long for me to realize I've taken a wrong turn somewhere. I'm no longer headed in the direction I took to get up to the top, and now I don't know where I am.

Another flash of lightning is no help. The shadows are shifting in the wind. And the rain keeps coming down.

CHAPTER TWENTY-SEVEN

Straining as hard as I can to see what's around me, I reach out and grab onto the trees on the other side of me to keep myself from slipping on the mud forming at my feet. Another flash of lightning accompanied by a tremendous clap of thunder startles me, and I take a step off to the side. The ground under me immediately gives way and my feet slip out from under me. The tree I'm holding onto cuts into my palms as I desperately cling to it, trying to regain my footing.

No matter how hard I struggle, I can't keep my grip. The rain is too hard, and soon my hands slip away. As I fall, I instinctively force my body around, so I'm sliding down a rocky ledge on my back rather than my more vulnerable stomach and face. I dig my heels into the ground to try to slow my progress, but it's no use. The ground disappears from under me.

I fall through emptiness for only an instant before my body hits cold, churning water.

The loud sound of the storm around me has blended with the torrential downpour of a waterfall. The pressure of the water hitting the surface creates a strong pull that drags me down. I push myself back up, desperately grabbing for breath. But as soon as I open my mouth at the surface, only more raindrops are dragged into my lungs.

The waterfall pulls me down again. I flail to orient my body and struggle to clear my brain. Rising up one more time for another breath, I relax to let the water bring me back down. Now that I've oriented myself, I finally open my eyes under the water. It's calmer somehow as if the storm cannot pass the thin line separating water and air. My heart is still racing, but I'm able to maneuver over and plant my feet on rocks positioned on either side of the waterfall. Pushing with every bit of strength I have, I propel myself away from where the waterfall drums down into the pool of water beneath it.

When I'm away from the force of the downpour, I surface and swim until my hands hit the edge, then pull myself up. Pain courses through me. My sinuses and lungs burn from the water I inhaled, but I'm on solid ground.

I drag myself painfully to my feet and look around as best I can. From what I can see, the waterfall flows down into an open area created by a horseshoe of rocks. It's not particularly high, but there don't seem to be any paths that lead up from where I am. There's no way my phone survived that, so I don't bother trying to fish it out of my pack.

Instead, I flatten one hand on the rocks and start to slowly walk around the narrow shoreline, hoping to find a pathway back to the resort in the darkness. I don't find a path, but after a while, I reach a large, flat rock sticking out from the wall a couple of feet up. Growling with effort, I drag myself up onto the rock. It's not much but it's progress.

It takes what feels like hours to climb up the side, going from rock to rock, occasionally slipping back down. By the time I get to the top of the cliff, I can hear voices somewhere through the pounding of the rain and the roar of the falls.

I scream out toward them, clawing my fingernails down into the ground to yank my body up. Hands clamp around my wrists and drag me up just as I feel like I'm going to fall again.

"Miss Griffin," a frightened voice says. "Are you alright? It's me, Joshua."

It takes me a few seconds to focus on the face in front of me. The rain has let up some, and I can open my eyes fully. It's the same older, friendly face that looked back at me through the rearview mirror on the drive to the resort. He has me by both arms, holding me up on my feet with more strength than I would have imagined from him. Relief washes through me, and I nod, resting my hands on the arms supporting me.

"I think I'm alright."

"Good, good." He turns his head over his shoulder to shout. "I found her! I have her!" He turns back to me. "What are you doing, Miss Griffin? Why would you come out here?"

"I didn't mean to," I tell him, shaking my head. "I went on a hike, and when it started raining, I got disoriented."

"You shouldn't be out here. *Cascada Esmeralda* isn't somewhere to come by yourself on a calm day. You come in weather like this, and you might just become a friend of the princess."

Before he can say any more, footsteps come crashing through the trees, and three people in bright yellow jackets appear. They guide me a short distance to a set of ATVs parked on a very narrow, rocky path leading down. Loaded into one of them, I rest my head against the roll bar and close my eyes, finally letting myself breathe.

Bellamy and Eric are at the infirmary when the vehicles arrive. They rush toward me, and Eric helps me out.

"What happened?" Bellamy asks frantically. "You were just supposed to go up onto the cliff and come back."

I nod painfully. "That's what I tried to do. But the storm started, and I got lost. I fell."

"When you didn't show back up, we called the lobby," Eric explains. "Catherine is the manager on duty, and she said they have a rescue team for the island. They sent them out looking for you."

"You need to get in and have the medic look at you," Joshua says.

I let him bring me inside, and while I sit on a table, drying myself with a stack of towels, the warm-eyed driver starts to leave.

"Wait," I say. He turns around with a questioning sound. "You're part of the rescue team?"

He's not wearing one of the bright yellow jackets of the other men. Joshua shakes his head.

"Not really. But I know the island like no one else. When I heard you were missing, I insisted they let me lead the search."

"Why?"

"There's something in you. I can see it. You're here for a reason."

It's more of the whimsical way he talked when we were on the drive to the resort, but it's strangely comforting.

"Can I ask you something?"

"Sure, you can."

He comes closer and sits on the chair next to the hard infirmary bed.

"That waterfall where you found me. What did you mean that I'd become a friend of the princess?"

"Yes. *Cascada Esmeralda.* Emerald Falls. The most beautiful falls on the island, but with the saddest story."

"Why?"

"Do you remember I told you about the people who once lived on this island?"

"You said they were frightened away by the ocean spirits. I thought that was just a tall tale you told for tourists."

"To the contrary, Miss Griffin. Those spirits have their roots deep in history. Long ago, this island was the home of a peaceful people. They once had a princess, beloved by the tribe. The language they once spoke is lost to us now, but she was named for the waterfall because her hair was long and beautiful and shimmering. We would call her Cascada now. She was beautiful and kind. Her father lavished her with attention. But her cousin, the daughter of the king's younger brother, was envious. She believed it should have been her father, who was in power. She wanted the attention, beauty, and adoration of the people."

"Sounds almost like a fairy tale."

"But the role of the princess was very highly prized in this tribe.

She was not just ceremonial. Her duty was to maintain the flame on the edge of the island, so passers-by from other islands would not crash into the rocks at night or in bad weather. This flame was always kept lit, rain or shine, no matter how bad a storm got. It was a princess's sacred duty to the people to watch over this flame.

"Shortly before she came of age, strangers arrived on the island. They were not from the surrounding islands but had come from far away. They were unusual, but they didn't try to hurt anyone and seemed interested in being at peace with the people of the island. One was a handsome young man who took a liking to both girls. The competition between the princess and her cousin was fierce, but the young man fell for Cascada. They fell in love. Her cousin was furious. Their romance was swift as the winds but as beautiful as the open sky. But he had to leave for his homeland. So when he departed, he gave her a beautiful emerald, with the promise that he would marry her upon his return."

"He left?"

"Yes. And he would never see his princess again. She stood on the cliff every day waiting for him to return to her, the flame lit both on the shore and in her heart to guide him back to her. She loved that emerald. She wore it on her forehead. She became the Emerald Princess. But months passed. Years passed. One day, Cascada saw his boat approaching. He had returned and would marry her! A sudden storm rolled in, not unlike the storm tonight. And the flame showing the way to safety had gone out."

"What happened?"

"She tried to get to it and relight the flame, but before she could, her sweetheart's boat smashed onto the rocks. She ran out onto the rocks just in time to see him drawn under the waves. Devastated, she went to her waterfall and threw herself in, wanting to join her love in the grottos. Many say her cousin was responsible for extinguishing that fire. Since then, the princess has sought to populate her new kingdom with any who may venture too close to her falls. That almost included you."

"What happened to the princess's cousin?" I ask, drawn into the story so much I barely notice the doctor checking the cuts and bruises on my arms, legs, and back.

"Everyone knew what she had done. Or at least wanted to punish someone for the loss of their beautiful princess. They brought her out to those rocks where the boat had crashed and killed her, then tossed her down into the water."

"The angry water spirit," I murmur.

Joshua makes a confirming sound and nods.

"You look long enough at those rocks; you'll see her trying to rise up out of the water. They say she's tormented by the princess and her love, able to see them but kept from them."

"What about boats?" I ask.

He looks at me with slightly narrowed eyes.

"Did you see a boat out there?"

"Yes," I nod. "At least, that's what it looked like. But nobody seems to know why it was out there."

Joshua shakes his head.

"You be careful, Miss Griffin. Boats don't go out there. They can't. Seeing a boat out there means you are seeing the crew of the princess's lost love, returning for vengeance against the island that killed them. None have seen that image and found a happy path off this island."

The doctor instructs Joshua to leave the room so I can undress, but before he leaves, the driver looks into my eyes.

"Be careful," he says. "Don't keep looking for the spirits, or they'll find you. The ocean spirits have claimed enough already."

CHAPTER TWENTY-EIGHT

An hour later, I'm finally back in my room, propped up in my bed with Bellamy sitting beside me. I tell her the story Joshua told me.

"It sounds like a fairy tale," she says.

"That's what I said. But almost every culture has them," I say. "And a lot of them sound really similar because they're based on the same themes. But he really seems to believe it. Like it's part of his understanding of the world around him. He says he knows the islands like nobody else does, that he comes from nearby. These must be stories that he's heard as he grew up."

"What do you think they mean?" she asks.

"I don't know. Obviously, I don't think it was a ghost of a distraught princess who killed herself that tried to get me down into that waterfall. But when I was standing on a cliff and looking at those rocks, the way the water moved was scary."

"What do you mean?" she asks.

"The waves crashed into them, and the water jumped up. That's the only way I can really describe it. It wasn't like it moves when it hits the other rocks. I can understand why people would be frightened by it," I explain. "What he said about the boats is what's really getting to me. I know I saw the boat out there. Twice now. But he says boats can't go out there."

"And you asked the manager about them?"

"Yes. And was told essentially the same thing. Boats don't go out there."

"What do you think that means?"

"I know what I saw. And tomorrow, I'm going to figure out why I did."

The next morning my body aches, but it doesn't keep me in bed. Getting up carefully, I cringe at the sore places and force myself into a shower. It doesn't do much to make the pain go away, but at least it loosens up my muscles so I can get dressed and head for the lobby. Catherine is walking across it just as I enter, and she immediately changes course to come to me, her expression worried.

"I heard what happened last night," she says. "Are you doing alright? Is there anything I can do for you?"

"I'll be fine. More embarrassed than anything," I tell her, trying to look sheepish.

"Don't be embarrassed. That area can be treacherous. I just can't imagine why you would be out there so late."

Her kindergarten-teacher voice makes me feel like I'm being scolded for going down the slide headfirst on my stomach.

"It was an accident," I offer. "My friends were out for the night, and I decided to take a hike to the cliffs. It was so peaceful the last time I was up there, and I just wanted some time to think. It's been a hard year for me. But then the storm started, and I got turned around."

"I'm very glad the team found you. That is not an area we generally encourage guests to go to. We don't block it off because the owner wants the island to be as accessible and natural as possible, but we leave it off the guide maps."

I tilt my head to the side with a curious expression.

"Really?" I ask. "That's strange because Alonso suggested I get instructions for how to find it."

"He did?" she asks, sounding surprised. The sweetness in her seems to falter just for a second before she picks it back up. "He must have gotten the impression you are an experienced hiker and could handle the terrain."

"Well, I certainly wish I'd found it on purpose," I tell her. "Happening on it that way isn't going to be my favorite vacation memory."

I'm trying to break the tension a bit, and it works. She smiles at me.

"I would certainly think not," she says. "And again, I'm so sorry you went through that. If there's anything I can do to help you."

"Actually, there is."

"Of course, what is it?" she asks.

"It's somewhat of a private nature," I tell her.

She nods.

"Absolutely. Come with me."

We cross the lobby, and she brings me down a long hallway to her office. Closing the door behind her, she motions for me to sit down.

"When I first went up to the cliffs, I thought I saw a boat far out in the water," I start.

She closes her eyes briefly and nods like she already knows what I'm going to say.

"Yes," she tells me. "Alonso mentioned that. Like he told you, we don't have any activities that go out that far in the water. That area is restricted access, and boats are not permitted near the rocks. It's an environmental issue."

"I understand that's the policy, but I saw the boat again yesterday. There is a security camera that covers an unused portion of the shoreline. Is it that area?" I ask.

Catherine looks surprised I know about the security camera but doesn't mention it.

"Yes," she nods. "We monitor that area to ensure no one from neighboring islands or who is traveling by will come ashore without us knowing they're here."

I nod. "That's what frightens me about the boat I saw. I know you told me there can't be any boats there, but I feel very anxious about the situation. You see, I've had a very challenging year, and it has put me into a bad headspace. My boyfriend went missing three years ago and resurfaced last year, but then was murdered."

"Oh my god," she says, her hand touching the necklace at her throat.

"As you can imagine, that experience had a serious effect on my feelings of personal safety. In fact, this is the first vacation I've taken since he disappeared. I really want to feel safe here because I enjoy it very much and would like to return. You may have noticed I've already lengthened my vacation. But if I can't feel secure and know I'm protected here, that's not something I can entertain," I tell her. "Which is very disappointing because I know a lot of people who would really love this resort. Some of the men have very particular tastes like men tend to do, and I think they would be happy here. But I can't honestly recommend it if I feel unsure about the safety."

"I fully understand that, and I want you to feel absolutely secure and at ease when you're here," Catherine says. "Would it reassure you to see the security camera footage?"

I let out a big breath and smile.

"Would that be possible?" I ask.

"Of course. Not a problem at all. Wait right here, and I will get it for you."

She leaves the office, and I snatch a business card from the holder on her desk, then run around to her computer. It's open, and I scan the icons on her desktop, hoping each of the managers has access to the same information. My heart jumps when I find the folder containing the guest's expense records. Moving as fast as I can, I email the entire file to myself. I then search for recent applicants and send myself that file as well, making sure to cover my tracks and delete the evidence from her outbox. I want to keep digging, but there isn't time.

I've just gotten back into the chair when Catherine opens the door again. She shows me a flash drive in her hand and goes around the desk to her computer. A flicker of confusion crosses her face when she looks at the screen. Shit. I must have left something up or not put the cursor back where she left it.

"I'm sorry," she says a second later, shaking her head and getting the smile back. "Our reservation system is acting up today, and I've been trying to figure it out."

Relief loosens my hand on the edge of my seat, and I smile at her.

"Technology can do that to you," I say.

"I swear, it's taking over," she laughs. "But anyway, I have that footage for you. Our security office gave me everything since you checked in. It's a continuous stream, but we can fast-forward so you can see everything."

She puts the flash drive in, and an image of a narrow, rocky beach appears on the screen. To one side is the rocky outcropping. The angle is different than I've seen it, but the footage covers the entire area, and I can clearly see the water in front of the rocks as well as out to either side and the front. Catherine leaves the video running for a few seconds. A few birds flutter by. A dolphin jumps through the water out in the distance. She scans through, and I stay focused on the water near the rocks. Minutes, hours, and then days pass, but the boat never shows up. When it's done, Catherine looks at me.

"Does that reassure you?" she asks.

"So much. It must have just been my eyes playing tricks on me."

"That happens. I'm just glad I could make you feel safer here. Is there anything else I can do?"

"Just one more thing. All this talk about water and boats has made me want to do some sailing. Can I arrange to rent a boat later?" I ask.

"Absolutely. But are you sure you're going to be up to it?"

"Definitely. I'm already feeling so much better."

CHAPTER TWENTY-NINE

As soon as I leave the lobby, I head for Emmanuel's room. He didn't specify a time, so I want to try to get in touch with him as early as possible. I knock on his door, but he doesn't answer. A couple more knocks get the same reaction. I'm getting ready for another round when the door two rooms down opens. A woman comes out and smiles at me.

"Are you here to see Emmanuel?" she asks.

"Yeah. He asked me to stop by. Do you know if he's here?"

"He goes for a jog and then swims every morning. I'm assuming that's what he's doing. I just checked in, but we've stayed here at the same time before. Takes a few hours, but he should be back later."

"Okay. Thank you."

She looks me up and down, and a bemused smile curves her lips.

"He's branching out," she comments. "I guess there's a spring sampler."

"Excuse me?" I ask.

She gives a dismissive laugh and pulls a pair of expensive sunglasses down over heavily made-up green eyes.

"Be careful. I heard swimming early in the morning can be dangerous for girls who know Emmanuel."

THE GIRL IN DANGEROUS WATERS

She breezes away, and I fight the sick feeling rolling in my stomach. The woman took the elevator, so I run into the stairwell and take the steps two at a time to my floor. I'm feeling it by the time I get there and slow down to a stiff limp as I head down the hallway. But I stop in my tracks.

The door to my room is standing open wide. My hand goes to my pocket before I remember my phone died a watery death last night. I'm about to turn around when I see a woman step out of the room. She's wearing a staff uniform, but her flaming red hair is not Graciela's.

"Hello," she says cheerfully when she sees me.

"Hi," I say, then point at my room. "You're taking care of my room today?"

"Yes, Miss Griffin. I'm Noelle."

"Where is Graciela?" I ask.

"I'm sorry, I don't know. Mr. Ordoñez assigned me your room this morning."

"Mr. Ordoñez— Alonso?" I ask.

"Yes. When I came to work today, he let me know I would be taking care of this block of rooms. I'm happy to help you with anything you need."

"Thank you," I say and step into my room. I'm about to shut the door when I stop. "Noelle, what rooms have you been taking care of?"

"I was assigned to the pool area. But I've been on leave for the last week, so I've been reassigned."

"On leave?"

"Yes," she says. "I was visiting my grandmother."

"That's nice," I tell her.

"Yes. She's been ill for some time, so it was good to see her. Let me know if there's anything I can do for you."

Noelle leaves, and I shut the door. Opening my computer, I pull up the emails I sent myself from Catherine's computer. Scanning over them, I take note of a few things, check the time, and send a message to Bellamy and Eric telling them to meet me in my room in two hours.

When I get out to the marina, the boat I rented is already waiting for me. A man who embodies everything that comes to mind when you think of an island skipper stands with one foot on the boat and the other on the docks, his hands on his hips as he peers at me through mirrored sunglasses.

"Miss Griffin?" he asks.

"Yes," I tell him.

"Perfect. Captain Alvin Ellison. This is your boat. Do you need any instruction?"

"No, I think I can handle it."

"Are you sure?" he asks. "I'd be happy to go out with you and give you a couple of lessons."

"No, thank you. I can do it."

Ellison nods and steps out of the way so I can get down into the boat. He hands a life jacket down to me, and I put it on, pulling the hooks snugly. After my night bobbing around in the waterfall, I'd prefer to have a leg up on the water should I end up in it. The captain starts the engine, and I take hold of the steering wheel. I've only controlled a watercraft like this a few times, but I feel confident enough to handle the brief trip I have in mind.

I head out into the water, purposely moving at an angle toward the cliffs I visited. I move further out into the ocean until I can glance over my shoulder and no longer see Ellison standing on the dock. Then I turn the boat and head in a large arc for the rocky outcropping.

I'm within a few yards of it when I notice what looks like plastic fencing marking off a section of the water surrounding the front of the rocks. It looks like the type of barrier used to mark off coral regrowth areas. A sign posted on a buoy a few feet away marks the area as a protected sanctuary and warns that boats are not permitted.

I notice something on the slope of rocks on one side leading down into the water, so I carefully ease just slightly closer. From that vantage point, I can see it's an oxygen tank, like the kind used in scuba diving. But I don't see a boat. Nothing's there.

I've been here long enough, so I turn away and drive the boat far out into the water so I can curve around and come back to the dock from the other direction. I stop it at the end of the dock, and the captain walks toward me with a quizzical expression.

"You're already finished?" he asks. "I thought you would be out there for a while longer."

"It's been a while since I've been on a boat," I confess. "I need a little more time to get my sea legs."

He laughs.

"Well, you know where to find me if you want to try again during your stay. You're always welcome."

"Thank you, Captain. You just may be seeing me again," I tell him.

I head back into the hotel and ride the elevator to Emmanuel's floor again. This time there's a Do Not Disturb sign hanging from his doorknob.

When I get back to my room, I'm hoping for another note from him, but there's nothing. I take a shower and change my clothes. I'm just coming out of my bedroom when Bellamy uses the extra key I gave her to open the door. She and Eric come inside, and she immediately comes over to me for a hug.

"Where were you today?" she asks. "I thought you'd be trying to recover from last night, but then I got your message."

"I can't just lie around," I tell her. "But since I don't have a phone right now, the best I could do is email you and let you know I'd be back later."

"Why couldn't you tell me where you were going?" she asks.

"Because I didn't want anybody to happen to see it or hear you talking about it," I tell her. "I spoke to Catherine this morning about last night. Apparently, the waterfall where I fell is one of the most dangerous places on the island, and they don't recommend guests go there at all. It's not on the guide map."

"But didn't you say Alonso told you to ask Joshua for instructions on how to get there?" Bellamy asks.

"Yes," I nod. "And evidently he does sometimes guide people there. But it's for really experienced hikers. I have a feeling a lot of those accidents on that report are from that area. I'm thinking maybe Alonso wanted to add me to it."

"Where did you go today?" Eric asks.

"I went to talk to Catherine about the boat I saw. Everyone I've spoken to says I could not have seen what I think I did. Even Joshua said boats can't be there. That I wouldn't have seen it, and if I did, it was some sort of bad omen that came from the spirits. So, I wanted to figure out what was going on. She mentioned the area is protected. So, when they say boats can't be there, they mean by law. Not because of anything that prevents them from coming."

"But no one else saw the boat," Eric notes. "I don't understand why no one else would notice it there."

"Because they don't think it would be. It's easy to miss something you don't think should be there. Think about the kind of clientele we've seen here at the resort. Can you honestly tell me you think a whole lot of them are avid hikers? How many do you think would go up on that cliff and spend a lot of time looking around? The boat isn't visible from the beach. You have to be up on the rocks in order to see it."

"Yeah, we were pretty high up," Bellamy chimes in.

"The driver Joshua goes up there. There are probably a couple of other people who work here who are from the neighboring islands who might. But every single one of them grew up with the legends about this island. Even if they did notice the boat, they wouldn't want to mention it. They wouldn't want to say anything and have people think they've somehow been cursed because of the boat."

"Do you really believe that?" Bellamy asks. "They must know it's just a story."

"Just a story or not, legends like that are deeply important to people. They're part of cultural identity, and even if someone knows for sure it's not true, there's still a part of them that wants to respect it. Those memories can really run deep. I mean, we can all claim we don't think Santa or the tooth fairy is real. But what do you do when some jolly old man in red shows up in your chimney?"

She nods like she understands.

"But Catherine isn't from any of those cultures. She would have no reason to not talk about a boat," Eric says.

"That's true, but again, she wouldn't see it if she didn't go up on the cliffs. She would have no idea it was even there. I told her I worried the resort wasn't safe, because maybe what I was seeing was someone who wasn't supposed to be here. Remember when I told you about the security cameras? I mentioned to her that I knew one of them covered an unused portion of the island. She admitted that was the section near those rocks. So she got me the footage for the last few days, and there was nothing. No boats, no people, nothing that got anywhere near that area," I tell them.

"So, there was no boat?" Bellamy asks.

"Not exactly. I rented a boat and went out there to see it for myself," I explain.

"Alone? Why would you do that?" Eric gasps. "You need to have someone with you."

"No, I don't. I need to be as unobtrusive as possible. The less you and Bellamy think I'm up to anything, the less the staff will pay attention to me. And it worked. They rented me a boat without question, and I went to see what was there. Like they said, there was a barrier saying it was a sanctuary, and no boats were permitted anywhere near as close as I saw the boat yesterday and the other day."

"But you just said you saw the footage," Bellamy points out. "Not only do you know there was no boat, but you know the cameras were there and were going to catch you being out there."

"Not exactly," I say. "From the footage I watched, security isn't going to get much information from the camera focused on those rocks."

"Why not?" she asks.

"There were no tides."

CHAPTER THIRTY

"No tides?" Eric asks.

"The water level never changed," I explain. "The video went from morning to night a few times, but the tide didn't go from low to high. It stayed at essentially the same level the entire time. But that's not how shorelines work. There are two low tides and two high tides every day. It takes a little more than six hours for the tide to go from its highest point to its lowest point, so the tide is at the same point a little more than twelve hours apart each time. But there was no evidence of that on the video."

"So, what's that mean? The security footage was hacked?" asks Bellamy.

"That, or it was manipulated," I say. "But not by someone who was paying very good attention. They wanted to control what the security team sees. They would need it to look like time was passing. But they didn't want them seeing what was really happening on that area of the island. So, they pieced together pieces of footage and created what I'm assuming is a very long loop. Several days' worth that look like they are a continually changing live feed but is actually just a recording. If I had to take a guess, there are other recordings to plug in when the weather changes, but it doesn't always work out. The footage I saw should have covered the storm, but the section of the night footage I saw didn't even have rain. It was only a few minutes of it, but there should have been massive lightning and pouring rain."

"Catherine showed you fake footage to prove there was no boat?" Eric asks.

"Right now, all I know is she showed me what security gave her. My thought is security doesn't even know the footage isn't real."

"What do you mean?" Bellamy asks.

"There are only a few security cameras here and they probably never record anything interesting. I doubt Desmond is sitting around watching the feed from the cameras all the time. More than likely, it's a lower-ranking member of the team. Probably too bored to even pay attention. The fake footage is a filler. It's just something to have up on the screen, so it looks like everything is fine over at the rock outcropping. Whoever rigged the system to show that footage all the time doesn't want anybody knowing what's happening over there. Including security."

"So, whoever put that footage in place has enough mechanical understanding to be able to rig the system, so it's undetectable by security. Not only are they watching it, but when they need to access footage from a particular time, what they pull up is actually from a recording, but it seems to be footage from the camera. That's fairly sophisticated," Eric says. "Somebody really doesn't want anybody to know what's happening over there."

"They don't want anybody knowing about that boat," I say. "That's where they're bringing the drugs in."

"So not everybody at the resort's in on it," Bellamy completes the thought.

"That's what it seems like," I nod. "They bring the boat up to that area and unload the drugs onto the beach. It goes unnoticed by anyone because security doesn't know about it, and the security camera is fake."

"Why don't you sound convinced?" Eric asks.

I shake my head.

"It's more than that. It's more than the drugs," I tell him.

"What do you mean?"

I look down at my hands, remembering the way the dirt looked under my nails last night after dragging myself up on the cliff. The image in my mind changes to Rosa's hand the morning we took her from the pool. The police dismissed the way one hand was curled like it was clamped around something, saying she must have grabbed onto the edge of the pool right before drowning. I still don't believe it.

Sitting down on the couch, I pull my computer close to the edge of the table and open it again to pull up the emails I sent myself.

"When I was talking to Catherine, and she went to get the security camera footage for me, I looked through her computer."

"Emma," Eric scolds. "You know you can't do that. We have absolutely zero jurisdiction here. The FBI doesn't hold sway over international waters.."

"Then I'm just a civilian," I tell her. "I'm not investigating on behalf of the Bureau, and I'm not here as a Sherwood deputy. I'm just a person who happens to know where to dig stuff up. Besides, I wasn't looking for evidence. I was looking for directions. And that's exactly what I found. Look at this."

Bellamy sits down beside me to look at the screen.

"What is this?"

"I emailed myself some of the files from her desktop. The incident at the spa interested me, and I wanted to check out the guest receipts to find out if anything stood out. They aren't just going to advertise it right there, but there has to be some way of keeping track. Not just for the cost, but also to keep track of the guests. Every good business knows you make more money from an existing customer than you do a new one. If you can learn what they like and keep it coming, you'll encourage more purchases and higher dollar investments."

"And what are these guests investing in?" Eric asks.

"At first the receipts look pretty normal. Just regular resort guest charges. Room services. Purchases in the lobby shop. Boat rentals. Tours. But then on some of them, I noticed a couple of odd notations. Right here," I point to the screen. "Spa, enhanced, A. Spa, enhanced, D. Spa, enhanced, H. Things like that show up over and over."

"There are different types of drugs available," Eric says. "It's noting the ones the person selected."

"Exactly. But those aren't the only notes. Look at these. C3. Three hours. Strawberry." I pull up a series of receipts one after the other to show them other notations. "C6. Two hours. Strawberry. C8. Two hours. Vanilla. C3. One hour. Chocolate. C3. Full. Special Request. C3. Half-hour. Special Request."

"C3, C6, C8. What are those?" Eric asks.

"Cabins," Bellamy says, realization settling over her. "It's talking about the cabins in the staff village."

I nod.

"Remember, I overheard that conversation between Alonso and Rosa. He said cabin three. None of the expense reports have the guests' names on them. That's not all that unusual. It's a privacy issue. And I'm sure the extra amenities offered by Windsor Palms requires additional privacy. What they do have is the room number. This one for cabin three is for room three-eleven. These two, the special requests, are for room five-o-two. That's the room Emmanuel Vargas is in. Those requests are the night that Alonso told Rosa had been requested, along with the day before she died."

"What do you think that means?" Eric asks.

"The note from Emmanuel gave me his room number and said 'tomorrow'. I went to his room this morning, but he didn't answer when I knocked on the door. A woman from down the hall came out of her room and said Emmanuel goes out for a jog and a swim every morning, so that's where he probably was. But then she looked at me a little strangely and mentioned Emmanuel must be trying something new. Something about a 'spring sampler'. I thought she was just being crass, but she mentioned she's been here the same time as he has before."

"She's seen him with other women," Bellamy says. "She must have known about him and Rosa."

"Not just Rosa, I would presume," I say. " But what about these other notations? Vanilla, strawberry…"

"Other codes for drugs?" she asks.

"Hair colors," I offer. "Blondes. Redheads. Brunettes. Special request."

"Well, that's tasteless," she comments.

"Not as tasteless as why they're describing them that way. Cabin three. Three hours. With a redhead. These women are being trafficked."

CHAPTER THIRTY-ONE

"The resort is providing guests with women as a special amenity?" Eric asks.

I nod.

"Think about it, B. When we went to the village, and we saw those girls."

"The housekeepers?" she asks.

"That's how we know them because it's the only service we want from them. But think about what we saw them do. They went into two of the cabins carrying the trays. One came right back out, but the other stayed. What did she look like? What color hair?"

"Dark," she says.

I scan through the expense reports active during that time and find exactly what I'm looking for.

"C12. One hour. Chocolate," I read.

"She had just come back from leave," Bellamy says.

"What? How do you know that?"

"I talked to her. I saw her at the pool and thought I recognized her. She was picking up towels and bringing clean ones to guys who were lounging around. Delivering drinks. That kind of thing."

"Pool duty," I nod. "The woman standing in for Graciela mentioned that she used to do that before she came back from leave and was reassigned to take care of the rooms."

"They have them on rotation?" Eric raises an eyebrow.

"That's what it seems like. They aren't just housekeepers. They do whatever the resort wants them to do. What did she say to you?" I ask.

"Obviously, I didn't say anything about seeing her at the cabins. I just talked to her about working here, and she mentioned it was so great, so many perks, on and on. She even specifically said she just started working here a few weeks ago and was already given leave."

My breath stabs at the insides of my lungs.

"Did she say what she was doing on leave?"

"She said she went to visit her grandmother…"

"Because she was sick, and it was nice to see her again," I continue, and Bellamy looks at me strangely.

"How did you know that?" she asks.

"Because it's the same thing Noelle told me. That's their cover story. Those girls aren't going on vacation. They aren't being given a break. They're being indoctrinated. Graciela said she'd never been offered leave and couldn't imagine why they would give the girls time off so soon after hiring them. That's why. The girls who are brought in to be trafficked work like it's a regular job for a week or two, then go on leave to go through training to become sex slaves. That van we saw at the dorm. It wasn't there for a delivery. It was a pickup. They were there to get the girls who were going into their training time. If I had to guess, I would say the drugs brought onto the island aren't just offered as extra amenities to the men here. They're used to control the girls, so they behave."

"And Rosa?" Eric asks.

"She didn't behave." I scan the emails again, then stand up. "I need to go back to the cabins."

"What if they catch you? I don't think they're actually going to believe you got lost if they find you poking around the cabins," Bellamy says.

"I'll have to figure it out if it happens," I answer.

"Do we need to act casual again?" Eric asks.

I shake my head. "No. This time you should come with me."

Walking into the bedroom, I pull my suitcase out and remove the small case from inside. I open it and piece my gun back together. This isn't just about Rosa anymore. Her murder is part of something much bigger, and I can't take any chances.

I thought it might be more anxiety-inducing walking toward the staff village during the day when so much is going on at the resort, but it actually seems quieter now. It occurs to me that the place is likely empty because everyone is working at the resort. They won't be in the village right now.

I still stay vigilant as we pass by the sign indicating that we are entering the staff only area and then walk through the gate and past the fence dividing the two areas of the island. We move quickly along the brick path to the cabins. There's no one around, and I go right for the cabin marked with a large three painted in white beside the door.

"What are you looking for?" Eric whispers as I step up onto the porch.

"Damage," I tell him.

"Damage?" Bellamy asks.

I nod and continue looking around. When I don't see anything, I drop down the steps and move to the back of the cabin. When Bellamy and I were behind the cabins, I noticed small patio areas behind the back doors. They weren't elevated like decks but had wooden barriers around the edges. Within a few seconds of searching the one behind the cabin, I find what I was searching for.

"Look," I say, running my fingers along three deep gashes in the wood. "Remember when we took Rosa out of the pool, and I saw her hand. It was clamped, and there was something under her fingernails. The police said it was from holding on to the side of the pool."

"Right," Eric nods. "The cadaveric spasm from right before she died."

"Yes," I say. "But it wasn't from the side of the pool. This is a woman who supposedly just smashed her head on the concrete and fell into the pool. How would she grab the side in that moment before she died? If she had that kind of strength, she could have pulled herself up, or at least turned over onto her back, so she was floating. She wouldn't have drowned that way. Her head injury was too bad for any of that. And the way her hand was, it wouldn't make sense if she was holding onto the side of the pool. The grip would be mostly in her fingers. But her whole hand was clenched, like it was holding on to something bigger."

"She grabbed onto the railing," Eric says, following along my theory. "Her fingernails dug into the wood."

"How did she get that gash in her head?" Bellamy asks. "There's no way she survived that long enough to get to the pool."

"She didn't," I tell her. "Her hand clenched that way the moment she died. And remember, there was no blood on the pool deck. I guarantee when the autopsy results come out, the cause of death will be blunt force trauma, not drowning. She'll have no water in her lungs because it was the blow that killed her. Right here. Someone bludgeoned her; I don't know what with, then brought her to the pool and dumped her in. They probably cleaned up the blood after so no one would notice, and then the rain took care of the rest."

"It seems like they could have done something better to make it look like an accident than put her in the pool. Even making it look like she fell on the rocks would have been less blatant and not call as much attention," she muses.

"But I think the attention is what they wanted. This wasn't an accidental killing that they suddenly had to figure out how to cover up. Whoever killed her wanted to make a statement. They put her in the pool so people would see her. That was the point of it. They were sending a message. She didn't do what she was supposed to do, and they wanted to make sure the other girls knew what happened if they did that."

"Do you think it was Emmanuel Vargas?" Eric asks.

"I don't know. If he killed her, why would he stay on the island? And why would he try to talk to me? I need to go see him and find out why he hasn't said anything to the police and what he was trying to tell me."

We get out of the staff village without being seen, and I leave Eric and Bellamy at the lobby while I go to the guest building. They're under instruction to request a phone for me and see if they can find out more about Graciela. I don't know what Emmanuel has to say yet, but just in case it could be valuable to Rosa's case or the rest of the girls, I don't want to spook him by showing up with two other people.

When I get up to Emmanuel's room, I notice the Do Not Disturb sign is still hanging on his doorknob. Ignoring it, I knock a few times and call in to him. The door of the room beside his opens, and a man sticks his head out.

"He's not going to answer," he says. "A couple of other people have come up, and he didn't answer them, either. I think he's sick. There was a terrible ruckus in his bathroom. For such an expensive place, the walls can be pretty thin."

"Thank you," I tell him.

Back in my room, I call Bellamy.

"Ask Constance about Emmanuel," I instruct. "Tell her I was supposed to talk with him today but haven't been able to get in touch with him."

I hear Bellamy ask and the musical response of Constance's voice in the background.

"She says he's sick," Bellamy tells me. "He called early this afternoon to ask for some medicine to be sent up to him. I asked who sent it to him, but Constance said Catherine told her only Paul was allowed to deliver to that room. That room is strictly off-limits to everyone else."

"Who's Paul?"

"One of the porters, I think," Bellamy shrugs.

"How about Graciela? Did she know anything?"

"She says she's not listed as being on leave. She just has a substitute listed beside her name."

"Okay. Tell her I say thank you."

At least I have that. Knowing Graciela is safe relieves some of the stress, but I still have those other women hanging over me.

Bellamy and Eric come into the room a few minutes later.

"They will have a new phone delivered to you by tomorrow," Eric tells me.

"Good," I say.

"What is it?" Bellamy asks.

"I can't stop thinking about that conversation we overheard at the dorm when we were behind the van. One of those voices said they had five, and the other said it was too many, that it would be noticed."

"But the other one said it was what the guests wanted," she continues.

"They were talking about the women they were taking," I say. "They are holding five women and teaching them to be sex slaves, and I have no idea where they are."

Eric looks into my eyes. "You have to take the lead on this one as a private citizen, Emma. I'll help in any way I can, but I can't get involved."

"I know," I tell him.

"What are you going to do?"

"Wait until dark and talk to the person who knows more than we do."

CHAPTER THIRTY-TWO

An hour later, it's dark enough.

Emmanuel specifically asked me to go to his room today to talk to him, and I haven't been able to get his attention. I don't buy his being sick enough to be unable to open the door. Whatever was important enough for him to need to talk to me isn't going to go away because he isn't feeling well. Something feels wrong. If he's not going to let me into the room, I have to find my own way in.

"Are you sure about this?" Bellamy asks as I step out onto my balcony.

"I can't think about it enough to decide if I am or not," I admit. "It just has to be fine."

I glance down to make sure there aren't a lot of people around. There is much of the same type of movement as every night, but the people are paying attention to each other rather than the building. I just have to hope they don't look up.

Going to the edge of the balcony, I lean back over the railing to count out rooms. When I've identified the balcony outside of Emmanuel's room, I climb up onto the railing. An unusual feature of the guest building is not working in my favor. The first time I saw the building, I noticed the balconies aren't lined up exactly like they are in most hotels. Instead, they are staggered, creating a less stark and generic appearance. Somehow the balconies not being an exact line makes the building blend in with the island environment more, as if the building itself is more relaxed.

But it's not the aesthetics I'm worried about right now. Instead, I'm focused on how the staggering of the balconies makes the distance between them harder to navigate.

I stand up on my toes and reach as far as I can, moving in slow, careful strides to the balcony just diagonal to mine. The door is dark, so I'm less worried about somebody being inside and noticing me pull myself up onto the balcony and walk across it. From there, I choose the next dark door I can access and drop down into it.

I make the mistake of looking down for a second while moving from one balcony to the next. I'm not on a skyscraper or anything, but I'm still several floors up. A fall from here would not be pleasant. A sudden dizzying sensation washes over me, but I take a deep breath. Relax, Emma. I redouble my grip on the wall and keep walking. The progress is slow, but eventually, I'm able to maneuver my way from balcony to balcony until I reach Emmanuel's room.

I finally reach his and scamper down from the ledge and sit down on the balcony, trying to regain my calm. I've never had to play Spider-Man during an investigation before. No one below started screaming about my being overhead or seeing me jump between the balconies, so I think I'm safe.

I stand up and go to the door. The curtain is pulled closed over the glass door, but I can see the glow of a light beyond it. I knock on the door, but there's still no response. The tip Graciela gave me the day I checked into the resort is the whole reason I'm on the balcony now. I need to get into Emmanuel's room, even if this is what it takes.

Obviously, whoever was taking care of Emmanuel's room didn't work at the resort long enough to know the trick to the doors. All it takes is a little pressure and a slight movement of the handle, and the door slides right open. I slip inside, and the second I move the curtain aside, I understand why Emmanuel didn't open the door when I knocked.

Blood is pooling in the middle of the floor, creating a trail through the room. It's not bright red, but a rusty brown, the results of oxidation after being exposed to the air for some time. Careful not to touch anything or step into any of the blood, I follow the trail through the room into the bedroom and to the master bathroom.

The door is partially closed. I use my elbow to nudge it open. Emmanuel is sprawled on the floor, the tile beneath him soaked in blood that seems to have flowed out of deep gashes stretching from the heels of his hands down to the middle of his forearms.

I take a step closer and note bruises on one upper arm and on the side of his neck. There is some redness on one cheekbone and a towel in one hand. Walking back out into his room, I notice the blood trail forking off. Smaller drops lead to the door that opens out into the hallway.

Lying just in front of the door is a menu. There's nothing I can do from inside the room. I don't want to touch anything, including the phone, and even if I was to call for help, me being inside the room without authorization could cause serious problems. I have to get back to my room.

The only way is along the balconies again. It's easier this time, with adrenaline fueling me. If someone sees me, I'll deal with the consequences of breaking into the room. It would cause complications, but that's not what matters right now. All I'm thinking about is getting to Eric.

He's already on his feet when I get back into my room.

"You need to call security," I tell him.

"What's going on?" he asks.

"Call Desmond and tell him you heard reports of noise in room 502, and after I haven't been able to get in touch with Emmanuel, you are concerned and want to run a welfare check. Pull the FBI card. Get pushy about it if you have to. You need to get in that room."

"Emma, what is going on?" he repeats.

"He's dead. I got into his room, and there's blood everywhere. He's on the bathroom floor, and his wrists are slit," I explain.

"He killed himself?" Bellamy asks.

I shake my head. "No. He's bruised, and the blood suggests a struggle. Even if whoever did this was trying to make it look like a suicide, they did a seriously piss-poor job of it. They got the direction of the wrist slitting right, but people don't generally slit their wrists in the living room and then make their way to the bathroom. There's also a towel in his hand."

"He was trying to stop the bleeding," Eric notes.

"He just never got a chance."

"I'll make the call."

Twenty minutes later, we're standing in Emmanuel's room again. Desmond and two other security guards stand back while Eric and I walk through the space. All three look drawn, more convinced than ever of their life choice to do security at a resort where they have little to do rather than actually going into law enforcement. None want to look at the blood. They keep their eyes focused on other places, occasionally looking at Eric or me, but not venturing closer to the body.

Eric takes pictures and speaks notes into the recorder on his phone. I get his attention to show him the menu at the door, and he takes a picture of it.

That's the image still in my head later when we're back in my room. The local police have come from the mainland to handle the newest death at the resort. Eric spent almost two hours with them after a couple of harried phone calls to Bureau higher-ups to get them started on the necessary paperwork as to not cause any legal issues.

It doesn't surprise me that their initial reaction is that Emmanuel killed himself. I've seen it before. Far too many times. But in this situation, it makes sense. Two staff members came forward during the initial investigation and mentioned the rumors about Emmanuel and Rosa. Though neither seemed willing to straight-out say they were having a relationship, there was enough suggestion and hearsay to all but confirm it.

Obviously, in his devastation after her death, Emmanuel couldn't take the grief and killed himself.

It's an easy conclusion for local police, but one that could be quickly discounted by investigators reviewing the case. They'll see the same things I did and know someone else was responsible for his death. What they might not see is the significance of the menu.

"Constance said he called for medicine this afternoon because he wasn't feeling well," I point out. "She sent some up from the infirmary. That can't be possible."

"Why not?" Bellamy asks.

"The menu on the floor is from this morning. Yesterday morning? I don't even know what time it is. It was on top of the blood. He was dead before he supposedly called for medicine."

"Could the menu have moved?" Bellamy asks. "Maybe he didn't pick it up, and the killer walking past it made it move into the blood."

I shake my head.

"Look at the way the blood is gathered at the top of the paper. It had already started to coagulate when the edge of the menu hit it and slid forward, gathering it. Emmanuel was dead before he supposedly called for medicine."

CHAPTER THIRTY-THREE

I'm starting out of the room when Bellamy stops me.

"Where are you going?" she asks.

"I have to go talk to Constance or somebody at the desk. Whoever can tell me who called for medicine, and who delivered it," I tell her.

"Emma, it's after two in the morning. You need to sleep," she says.

"No, I need to find out what happened."

"You do need some rest," Eric insists. "Even if there is someone in the lobby right now, it's not going to be the same people who work in the morning. They might not even know who handles something like that. You need to get at least a couple of hours of sleep before you do anything else."

"Fine," I finally relent.

"Good," he says. "We're staying here in the room with you. You're not going to be alone at night until we figure out what happened."

I want to argue with him, but he's right. Someone killed Emmanuel, and I can only imagine it's because of what he knew. It's not going to take much for them to know I'm unraveling what's going on here at the resort, and that means I'm dangling by a thread.

Eric gets an extra pillow and blanket and stretches out on the couch in the living area while Bellamy comes into the bedroom with me. It doesn't take her too long to fall asleep, but I lay awake, staring up at the ceiling, trying to make sense of everything. Finally, I can't take it anymore and climb slowly out of bed. Moving as quietly as I can as to not wake up Bellamy or Eric, I get my computer and curl up in a chair.

I send an email to Sam, promising to call him the next day to explain everything. Even though I don't get to hear his voice, somehow, just sending him a message is comforting. I close my computer and climb back into bed. This time I'm able to drift to sleep, but it's thin and fitful. I only manage to scrape together a couple of hours over the rest of the night.

I'm startled awake by the sound of someone knocking on the door. For a brief second, the thought that it must be Emmanuel flashes through my mind, quickly chased by the reality of what happened last night. I'm out of bed in an instant and throw on the first clothes I can get my hands on. By the time I open the door to the bedroom, I hear voices coming from the front of the room.

"Oh, good morning. I came to speak with Miss Griffin."

"You can speak to me," Eric says.

But he doesn't need to defend me. The second I heard those words, I knew who was standing on the other side of the door. I'm across the room in a flash. Alonso's eyes widen slightly when he sees me, and I grab him by the front of his shirt to yank him into the room as I kick the door closed.

"Where are they?" I demand.

"Emma," Eric warns, trying to step up to me, but I maneuver around him and force Alonso further into the room.

"Who?" the manager asks.

"You know who I'm talking about," I snap. "Where do you have them?"

"I don't know what you're talking about. I came to check on you."

Eric carefully disengages my hands but keeps himself positioned between Alonso and the door. It's a careful balance, not wanting me to lose control, but also not being willing to let him get away.

"Check on me?" I ask incredulously. "Why? Because you wanted to see how much I figured out?"

"I don't know what you're talking about," he says again. "I was worried about how that man's death might be affecting you. Desmond let me know you aided in the investigation."

"Yes," I tell him. "I did. It only felt right considering Emmanuel— which was his name, by the way— Emmanuel, not 'that man', was going to tell me what he knew about the girls."

"What girls?" Alonso asks.

He moves out of the way as I lunge toward him.

"Drop your act."

His eyes flicker back and forth like he's trying to find someone who can help him.

"Are you asking about Graciela? I don't know where she is. I'm as shocked as anyone about what happened," he tells me, doing his best impression of honesty.

"What do you mean about what happened? Noelle told me she took a couple of days off."

"She wrote me a note," Alonso says. "It said she was going back home to help her family, that her mother said she needed her."

I fall back a step, my hands coming up to cover my mouth as my head shakes.

"They have her," I mutter.

"What is it, Emma?" Eric asks.

"Graciela didn't take a couple of days off. They have her. Wherever the other girls are, they have her. She never would have quit this job. Especially not like that. Coming to work here on this island was her dream. There's no way she would have just walked away from it. And her mother wouldn't have told her she needed her help. Her mother is the one who encouraged her to go out into the world and follow her own dreams. She's the one who told her to be true to herself and go out and make the most of herself. Whoever wrote that note didn't know her well enough," I say.

My teeth clench so hard my jaw hurts as I turn back to Alonso. "Where is she?"

"I told you, I don't know. I got that note and that's it. I haven't been able to get in touch with her."

"You need to stop pretending," I tell Alonso, my voice made of gravel. "You aren't convincing anyone. I know this resort is a cover. You're offering your guests the same drugs you're using to keep control over the women you're treating like bottles of liquor in a minibar. You churn them through your little prostitute training academy, then turn them out to entertain your VIP guests. Six of them are being held right now. The five you have marked as being on leave and Graciela. I don't know how you got your hands on her, but she better not be hurt. Tell me where they are."

"You have to believe me when I tell you I don't know what you mean."

"I don't have to believe a word that comes out of your slimy mouth. You need to stop thinking about your cover because I already know it isn't true. What you should actually be worried about is that if there is a single hair hurt on any of those women, I will personally see to it that you are put on a small platform and gradually lowered into prison while guards announce that you traffic women and pump them full of drugs to keep them compliant. Then they'll bring you back up, let you recover a bit, then dip you back down. Over and over again until there's nothing left to bring back up. Do you understand me?"

Alonso cracks, his face going red then pale and his hands shaking.

"Okay, I'll admit it. I know about the drugs. They're offered in the spa and lounge, and to specific vetted guests in their rooms."

"Or the cabins?"

"Yes. Occasionally our elite guests will want more privacy and will request one of the cabins for the night. Their choice of drug is delivered to them there along with anything else they might require."

"Like a woman who fits their description of choice?" I ask.

He shakes his head hard.

"No. Nothing like that. All I know about is the drugs. I don't know who orders them or how they get here. All I'm responsible for is collecting guest requests, ensuring they are authorized, and having their choice delivered to them. Yes, that is done by the women on the staff, but that's it."

"Get off it, Alonso. I heard you talking to Rosa. You told her a guest was renting cabin three for the evening and that you wanted her to fulfill his expectations."

"Mr. Coltrane," he replies with a nod. "Three lines, a bottle of whiskey, classical music, and fruit tarts. It's the same thing every time he visits. The last time he was disappointed because the room was not set up to the specific way he requested it, and it had to be redone, which cut into his time. I was emphasizing to Rosa that she needed to be prompt and ensure everything was done the right way. No one else was in that cabin with him."

"You talked to Frederick about the girls going on leave," I point out.

"The women who are on leave are taking time off from work. It's part of the benefits offered to them when their manager hired them."

Alonso sounds confused, and his wide eyes are getting bloodshot.

"Graciela was never offered leave."

"I know that. It's not something I offer when hiring new staff."

That strikes me.

"You didn't hire Rosa?" I ask.

"No. She was brought in by the staffing company."

"What staffing company?"

"The resort is constantly looking for new staff, exactly like I told you. Many of the people who come to work here think it sounds amazing until they understand the full pressures and responsibilities."

"Like being expected to fulfill the sexual requests of strangers?" I ask.

"No," he says firmly. "Being away from home. Not having access to social media, as is the policy of the resort for all staff. The formality and standards. It's easy to think working on an island will just be about partying and relaxing, but that's not what is required of our staff. Those who leave have to be replaced, and we like to have a larger staff than we need to ensure there is never a guest left waiting. A staffing company is used to fill those spots in addition to hires by the resort itself.

"Oh, God," I gasp, looking at Eric. "The note from Emmanuel. It said, 'he didn't hire her.' He was talking about Alonso. Alonso didn't hire Rosa. Graciela must have told him I asked about the two of them talking. He wasn't having a relationship with her. He was trying to warn her. Rosa had probably agreed to leave, and he was trying to help as many others as he could."

CHAPTER THIRTY-FOUR

"Rosa's death wasn't accidental," Alonso gasps as the words formed in his head.

"No, it wasn't," I explain. "Just like I told you the morning she was found. She was murdered. Somebody bashed her brain in and tossed her in the pool to send a message. Every other one of the girls being trafficked through here saw that and knew what it was. She said the wrong thing. She was trying to get out, and they wanted to make sure no one else tried that. And the only man around here who cared got beaten and his wrists slit for it."

Alonso's legs buckle beneath him, and he drops down to sit on the couch behind him. He puts a hand to his mouth in shock but doesn't say anything.

"He stayed here to try to help. He wanted to tell me what was going on, and the disgusting people treating these girls worse than animals slaughtered him to make sure every other man who ever stepped foot in this resort knows to keep his mouth shut. And the same thing is going to happen to every one of the other girls if you don't tell me where to find them."

"I don't know," he sighs. "I would never do something like that."

"You'll traffic drugs but not girls?" I ask.

"Yes," he says emphatically. "A person who wants to do drugs is making a personal choice. It's recreational. Something to enhance their trip. Many of our clients come from all over the world, where such drugs are perfectly legal. This is not the United States. I don't do it, but it's not my choice. It's theirs. But I would never sell them a person."

"Then what was that nonsense about suggesting I go to what is apparently the most dangerous place on the island? You were going to send me up there, hoping I would get hurt and wouldn't be able to talk about what I was uncovering?" I say.

Alonso shakes his head, looking down at his lap.

"No," he says. "I know Cascada Esmeraldas well. Yes, it can be dangerous for those who don't know the area. But it's also the most beautiful place on the island. I wanted you to ask for directions on how to get there because I was going to meet you up there once Joshua gave you the directions."

I'm not sure how to process what he just said.

"Why?" I finally ask.

His eyes lift to me.

"Because I'm interested in you, Emma. I didn't know how to approach you. I thought if you went to the falls and I was there, we could spend some time alone together. I could show you around and tell you the stories of the island. We could get to know each other better," he says.

"The stories of the islands," I say under my breath as thoughts streaming through my mind drag my focus away.

"What?" he asks.

My eyes snap to him.

"Frederick was giving the new staff the tour of the resort. Is he the contact with the staffing company?"

Alonso nods. "Yes."

"Who puts the menus under the door every morning?"

"Paul. That's just one of his responsibilities. He helps with luggage, does deliveries, escorts the female staff, generally whatever is needed."

"And is he the one who delivered medicine to Emmanuel's room after he'd died?"

Alonso shakes his head.

"I'm not sure."

"It must have been him. According to Constance, Paul is the only one allowed to deliver to Emmanuel's room."

Alonso cocks his head curiously and frowns. "What are you talking about? We've never had a rule like that. Maybe if you ask who was on duty yesterday."

"Constance told Bellamy, Catherine gave her the instructions," I tell him.

"Catherine?" he asks.

"Crap." I cover my eyes with my hand and shake my head. When I take my hand down, I look intensely into his eyes. "You need to listen to me carefully because I am doing everything I can right now to see the humanity in you and give you the benefit of the doubt. It is not easy and trust me when I tell you if you take even the slightest step out of line, I will make you wish to be dipped into the general population. And be assured that is not a threat; it is a disclaimer."

"What do you need?" Alonso asks.

"I need to figure out how they are pulling this off, and you're going to help me. If you do, I'll think about what I'm going to do about your role in everything. You don't want to go down for human trafficking. Running drugs is not worth lives, and whatever it is you get out of being a part of this, it's not worth the risk."

"I'll help you."

I nod.

"How quickly does Frederick process girls? When he finds one he wants, how long does it take him to get her here and put her on leave?" I ask.

"I've seen him get an application and have the girl here by the next day," he says. "He always says it is because of her 'unique offerings'."

"She's a special request," I say, remembering the wording on the expense reports. "So, if I was able to ensure that a specific girl applied for a position here and fit the description for a very wealthy VIP client, you think he would be willing to expedite her getting to the island?"

"That's possible," Alonso said.

"What if she is already a guest here? Has he ever hired someone right off the island?"

"Yes. There have been a few occasions when he offered an on-the-spot position after he was particularly impressed by a girl he saw at the pool or on the beach."

"Or after a high roller put in a request," I say. "Let's see how loud money talks."

"What do you need me to do?" Alonso asks.

"Get me an application for the staffing company. Make sure it will go to Frederick so he will hire her. When a reservation comes in for Sam Johnson, talk him up. Make him seem extremely important and powerful. Someone Frederick would want to have on his list of VIP guests."

"I can do that. What else?"

"Keep your mouth shut. Go about everything like normal. Don't say a word about Rosa. Don't say a word about Emmanuel. Cooperate with the police, no matter what they say about his death. And tell me where to find Joshua."

By the time my new phone is delivered to my room, Alonso is gone. I call Sam, and as much as I want to listen to him tell me how much he misses me and what he's been doing, I have to stop him. Staying as calm as I can, I tell him everything that's happened and what I figured out. When I get to the part about Alonso leaving, he makes a sound that is almost unapproving.

"What?" I ask.

"Are you sure you can trust him? You just let him walk out?"

"I had to," I explain. "When it comes right down to it, the choice is between saving those women and knocking him on his ass for the drugs. Women will win every single time. If I ever have to choose between shutting down a drug trafficking or a human trafficking ring, the drugs aren't even going to register. I'll deal with that when I know those six women are safe."

"What do you need me to do?" he asks.

"Remember how I was uncomfortable with Greg leaving me his money and his life insurance?"

"Of course," he says.

"I found a good way to use it. We're going to have to cut our Christmas vacation a little short this year. You have a plane ticket in your email right now. I'm sending you contact information for the resort and exactly what you need to say. You'll be speaking directly to Constance to make your reservation. Be sure to emphasize that the resort comes highly recommended for your particular taste and that you have a specific special request you want to be fulfilled. Say you are interested in having strawberries and cream in the cabins and are willing to pay a premium to ensure you get the juiciest one."

My stomach turns, and I nearly gag just saying the words. I'm thankful he doesn't have me repeat them. The combination of the words used to describe the women on the expense reports and the code Alonso told me is used when making the drug transactions should be enough to put Constance at ease.

"You have no idea how hard it's going to be for me to be at that resort and not be able to talk to you," he says. "As soon as I see you, I'm going to want to scoop you into my arms and take you away somewhere where no one will be able to find us for a few days."

"I already extended my vacation here," I tell him. "But after two murders and the revelation of a drug and human trafficking ring, I highly doubt that reservation's going to be honored. But maybe we can find somewhere else when this is all done."

"Or we can just have a staycation at home," he offers.

"Deal, as long as you never use the word staycation again."

He gives a soft laugh, the strained kind of chuckle that comes from knowing the situation around us is brutal, and we have to search for any shred of humor to get us through.

"I love you, Emma," he says.

"I love you, too, Sam. Be careful."

We get off the phone, and I wipe a tear from my cheek before turning to Eric.

"Did you get her?" I ask as he hangs up his phone.

He nods. "Mallory Harding. From the Miami Bureau office. Five-foot two, red hair, petite and delicate. She'll be here tonight."

"Perfect. So will Sam."

"What are you going to do now?" Eric asks.

"I need to talk to Joshua."

CHAPTER THIRTY-FIVE

"Tell me again about the princess we could call Cascada."

The old man sits outside the small shack built outside the staff village. When I first arrived, he explained he is the only member of the staff of the resort who does not live on the island full time. He barely even considers himself an actual employee of the resort. Instead, he feels like he works for the island. His responsibility is to bring people from the tiny private airport to the resort and back, but he takes it on as his duty to protect the island he loves.

Joshua takes a bite of the fruit cut into a bowl in his lap and lifts his eyes to me.

"This is about the man who died," he notes.

"Yes," I say.

"The ocean spirit is angry," he says. "He loved that girl the way the princess was loved."

"Joshua, I researched the islands. I can't find anything about why that area is protected. I see that a long time ago, it was considered a historic area, but I can't find anything about actual environmental protections being in place, or what that sanctuary should be for. What else could be protected there?"

He shakes his head. "I don't know. I don't go over there."

"Because of the ocean spirits?"

"Because it's dangerous," he shrugs.

"Tell me about the princess again," I say. "You mentioned grottos."

"Yes," he says. "She and her love reunited in the grottos and will live out their eternity there together."

"But the angry ocean spirit can't, right? That's what you told me?" I ask.

"She's kept from them," he says.

"Joshua, are the grottos real?"

I try to say the words carefully, not wanting to offend him but needing to make sure there was a difference between the legend and reality. I like listening to his stories, but right now, I need the truth.

"Yes," he says.

"Real like they could be on a map of the island?" I ask.

"Miss Griffin, just because a story may be hard to believe, doesn't make it any less true. Stories are passed down for generations. They turn from stories into lessons. Ways of explaining the world to make things easier. Maybe the original meaning is lost. But a story about the lovers living together in eternity while the jealous one suffers makes the world easier to live in, do you understand?"

"I do," I tell him.

He nods. "Good. Yes, the grottos are real. But they are extremely difficult to get to. Cascada is believed to be in one because when she jumped into her falls, her body was never recovered."

"Have you ever shown anyone how to get to the grottos?"

"No. I've never been there myself. But the old folks of my time used to say anyone brave enough to find them could live their entire lives in them."

"So, it's not a small place?"

"No."

"Thank you, Joshua."

I spend the rest of the afternoon researching the island. There isn't as much about it as I would like for there to be. Because it is a private island, and apparently has been for quite some time, extensive mapping is limited. What needs to be done is something that can only be done once, so I need to be absolutely sure I'm right.

I'm packing my supply pack in my room that evening when Alonso appears at my door again. I'm almost uncomfortable now that I know about his attraction to me, but he only lets his eyes linger on me for a second before we go inside.

"I just wanted to let you know Frederick has already seen Agent Harding and has taken notice of her," he says. "She will be in room 312."

"Good," I nod. "Was Sam able to get a reservation without a problem?"

"I spoke to him briefly, and he said that there was some resistance until he used the words you told him to use, then Constance happily gave him a room."

I nod, feeling uncomfortable about having to connect Sam and Alonso to handle the details of what I'm planning. As much as I hate it, I need to stay as distant from Sam as possible until this is done. I can't afford for anybody to know we're connected, and he needs to work closely with Alonso to ensure he does and says everything he needs to in order to fit the narrative. I keep telling myself this won't be forever. It will be over soon enough.

"When will he put in the request?"

"Soon," Alonso says. "We agreed he would add urgency to the request by saying how lonely he is to be here at night alone. Then he will describe his ideal girl and offer a premium to have that description fulfilled." He looks at his watch. "Bellamy is down by the pool by now. Are you sure about this?"

"Yes," I tell him. "Just keep them away as long as you can."

"I will do my best," he promises. Tossing my bag onto my back, I give him a single nod and move quickly out of my room. Pain still echoes through my body, but I force it down and ignore it. I managed to get into Emmanuel's room; I can do this. I have to do this. There's no choice. This is my one chance, the one opportunity I have to save six women.

Joshua's boat bobs at the edge of the water. I asked him not to bring it up to the dock, but to leave it near the pier at the bottom of the rocks where it would stay safe, but where nobody would see me disembark. I need to be as invisible as I possibly can.

This boat is much smaller and older than the one I rented from the resort, so it takes longer to drive out into the water and make the large curve that will keep me out of sight. The water is smooth and clear, almost eerily calm despite the hammering in my heart.

I make my way to the outcropping of rocks and the strange sanctuary sign that seems to mean nothing. The oxygen tank I saw on the rocks the first time I was there is gone. It tells me exactly what I needed to know. I anchor the boat to a nearby rock and bring the engine to a stop.

Kicking off my shoes, I peel away my clothes and change quickly into my wetsuit. Bracing myself and putting all my trust in my instincts, I stand up. The small boat rocks and moves under my feet, but I'm able to gain enough purchase to gather myself and take a deep breath.

I lower my mask and snorkel over my face and plunge down into the water.

My eyes open. Everything around me is dark. I turn on the flashlight strapped to my arm. The waterproof device came right out of Alonso's emergency supply kit and creates what feels like a protective glow around me.

It takes only a matter of seconds for me to see the gap in the rock wall in front of me. The water moving over it causes the waves to jump up and spray more aggressively than they would without the gap. A shock of trepidation goes through my chest, but I don't hesitate.

I kick as hard as I can, propelling myself down toward the gap, and squeeze through. Panic is starting to set in slightly. Even though I know I'm safe, fear is pressing in around me, making me want to take a breath. I feel desperate to rise up to the surface. But I can't. I'm surrounded on all sides by rocks. I'm too deep now to come up for air. There's no way out but forward.

I follow the hazy beam of light through the underground tunnel for what seems like forever, pushing and straining every muscle to try to get through. My lungs are burning. My heart is racing. But I have to keep going. Those women are depending on me.

And then the pressure is suddenly gone. The rocks give way, and I shoot upward to the surface. My lungs fill joyfully, desperate for every tiny amount of oxygen I can give them. I rip the snorkel out of my mouth and take a few deep breaths as I drift toward an edge.

The flashlight reveals what I'd expected: I'm in an underground chamber with water filling the bottom and a towering ceiling. I swim over to the edge and climb out. I look around every which way, but there's only one place to go. Ahead of me is a natural tunnel. I shine my light into it to make sure there's nothing in my way before continuing through. Down here is colder, and I shiver, goosebumps rippling up through my skin.

Finally, I step out into another chamber. This one is more like a cave, the water creating just a small pool in the center. All around it are rock formations. I don't need my flashlight here. Enough glow comes from the oil lamps hanging from hooks in the stone walls. That same glow touches on the terrified faces of women chained to the stones.

They look dazed, not fully aware of what's going on. But Graciela lifts her head, and her eyes hit me. For a second, it seems like she doesn't recognize me like she doesn't actually believe I'm there. Then her eyes widen.

"Miss Griffin," she whispers.

"Emma," I tell her. "Don't worry. I'm here."

"I am so happy to see you," she gasps. "I don't know what's happening. I don't know how I got here."

"Graciela, listen to me. I'm with the FBI. I'm investigating what's going on at the resort. I'll explain everything to you later," I tell her. "But right now, we need to focus on getting all of you out. Where's the key to your chains?"

"He keeps it with him," Graciela says.

"Who? Frederick?" I ask.

"Yes," she nods. "He brought us down here."

"Did he take you from the village?"

"No. It was Paul."

"Paul took you?"

She nods weakly. "Paul is their muscle. He took all of us. He is the one working with Frederick."

"And he's the one who supposedly delivered medicine to Emmanuel's room," I mutter.

I look around to the other terrified faces and sigh deeply.

"I am so sorry to have to do this to you," I say. "But I am going to have to leave you here and be right back."

"No," she pleads desperately. "I can't be down here anymore."

"I can't get you out of your chains," I say. "You have to trust me. I will send someone back for you as soon as I can. I promise."

"You aren't going to come back?" she asks.

"There's something I need to do. But I promise I'll see you soon. A team of FBI agents is coming to get you out of here, I promise. It won't be much longer. Then you'll never have to face any of this again."

CHAPTER THIRTY-SIX

I wish I had taken the time to blow dry my hair. It hangs cold and still damp against my back. My hair has always been so thick it clings to water and stays wet for hours if I don't dry it. Now it presses between the soft cushion of the chair and my shirt, the cold wetness seeping through and sending chills down my legs. But I don't move from where I'm sitting. The back of my chair is to the hotel room door, and I stare out into the darkness beyond the balcony.

Only the glow of the night light in the bathroom at the end of the bedroom creates shadows in the illumination in the room. I've been sitting here in Room 312 for almost an hour, the anticipation tingling up my legs and in my fingertips. My heart beats hard enough for me to feel it in my stomach and taste it on my tongue.

It seems as if I keep doing this. Placing myself as bait to wait for someone to come. I don't mind doing it. I'm a trained fighter, and I can more than hold my own. Sure, I could call the police to do this. But I don't have time for that now. And I don't know if I can trust them.

No, if someone's going to take down Paul, it has to be me. And if I have to be the bait, I'll do it.

The sound of the door handle behind me makes sparks of color jump behind my eyes and burst into my brain. I ready myself, staying as still as I can and concentrating hard on controlling my breaths, so I'm silent in the living area.

The figure slips into the room, and I watch him in the faint reflection on the glass. For a second, I wonder if he can see me, too. The small bit of light from the bathroom might not be enough. But I can't change it now. He stands there for a second, staring at the door, and I close my eyes.

If he can see my reflection, I don't want him to see that my eyes are open. Straining for sound, I listen for his footsteps to cross the room and come closer to me. My muscles twitch. I have to time this exactly right. Not too soon, definitely not too late.

Finally, his footsteps are loud enough for me to know he is within only a couple of feet from me. Jumping up from the chair, I throw off the blanket that was draped over my lap, step up on the cushion of the chair, and launch myself over the back and onto him.

I get the drop on him with a hard cross to his jaw. Paul stumbles backward, obviously stunned, and I grab for my handcuffs to lock onto one of his wrists while he is still confused. I slam the cuff down on one wrist, and it spins over to lock into place, but I can't tighten it before he rushes into me, shouldering me back and against the wall.

I try to keep my feet under me but slip and hit the ground. I see a syringe roll from his hand under the door to the bathroom. His eyes dart over to it as well. We both lunge for it, but I get there first, slamming the door onto his fingers and getting a roar of pain from him before I jam my elbow into his nose.

I don't know exactly what's in that syringe, but I absolutely do not want to find out. It needs to stay far out of the way. I try to position myself between him and the door to make sure of it, but he is already up and back at me again. Paul's frame is massive, and despite his size and strength, he is deceptively quick on his feet, and he uses one of them to kick me hard in the ribs. I fly back into the door and hear it creak under the sudden weight of me hitting it.

Paul takes a step back and then charges shoulder first at me. I try to dodge it, but his arm extends to his side, and he tackles me as we both plow into the door. It explodes off the hinges. Splinters rain down as the door cracks and crumbles beneath us. We land with a crash on the bathroom tiles.

Paul is grabbing frantically, searching for the syringe, and I take the chance to smash him hard in the face again, aiming for his swollen, bloody nose. A direct hit makes him wince and pull back his fist. He slams it down, but I move my head in just enough time for him to put a hole through what remains of the door. I grab at his eyes as his weight presses down onto me, keeping me from being able to escape or grab something to use as a weapon.

As I claw at his face, one hand grabs for my throat, and he clamps down hard. I can feel my windpipe being squeezed. I know it's only a few moments before he will choke me out. Suddenly a searing pain rockets across my cheek, and I realize he is punching me with the handcuff around his fist.

My arms feel weak, and I have a hard time flailing at him. He hits me again, hard. Blood bubbles up in my mouth, and I spit out a stream of it onto his hand, still wrapped around my throat. I roll my head to the side to see the fist that has punched me is clenched around something else now. Panic runs up my spine.

The syringe is jammed into my shoulder before I can react, and I kick wildly when it goes in. One of my flails hits him low, and he crumples a bit, giving me just enough room to wiggle out from under him. Adrenaline pumps through my body to counteract the drugs I know are going to hit me any second. I grab the arm that had been choking me, wrapping my legs around it. Popping my hips, I am able to get my body weight pinned between the doorframe and the bathroom sink. There is nowhere for him to go, and his elbow is being bent at such an angle that all it takes is for him to move the wrong way by just an inch and...

He howls in pain as his elbow snaps. I let go of him and hop onto his back. Wrapping my arms around his neck from behind, I cinch up hard, pressing my knee into his lower back. With only one arm and on his stomach, he is helpless. I hold him tight under the chin, constricting his breathing with both arms until I hear him snoring in my grip. When I let go, his face smashes into the tile, and I wipe my mouth with my sleeve before yanking the handcuffed wrist over to the toilet. I snap the other side of the cuff around the pipe bolted into the wall and stand up, trying to catch my breath.

With Paul finally handcuffed, battered, and bloodied, but no longer coming at me, I drag myself up and into the bedroom where I left my phone, gasping for breath. I purposely didn't want it in the room with me where I was waiting. It was too much of a risk that he'd see the phone and destroy it. The only landline in the room is in the bedroom, but I wanted to be able to quickly call the contacts I had in place.

My vision blurry and breathing labored, I grab it and hit the first number saved.

"Are you alright?" Sam asks as soon as he picks up.

"Please just come," I gasp.

"Be there in a second."

The call drops, and the dizziness takes over. Drawing in a deep breath to try to flush my body with oxygen, I head back into the living room. Every step is wobbly, and the room seems to tip back and forth as I walk. Flattening my hand on the wall, I feel for the light switch and hit it. The lamp bursting on stings in my eyes. I feel like it almost physically knocks me back.

Grabbing onto the back of the chair, I hold myself up and keep my eyes trained on the doorframe to the bathroom, waiting for any sign that Paul might try to break out. Fortunately, it's only a few more moments before the door opens, and Sam runs inside. I let go of the back of the chair to open my arms to him. Just as he reaches me and goes to take me into his arms, my legs collapse, and I fall into darkness.

* * * * *

I wake up to the sharp smell of antiseptic and the harsh feeling of gauze against raw, open wounds. Sam's is the first face I see, and I nearly cry with happiness. He cups his hand against my cheek, and I tilt my face into it, kissing his warm skin.

"What happened?" I ask.

"He got you with his syringe," Sam says. "The sedative intended for Agent Harding got into you. But you managed to fight it off before the full dose. You were able to stay functional long enough to fight him off before the adrenaline wore off and the drugs kicked in. But once you had him cuffed and called me, everything shut down."

"How long have I been out?"

"A few hours," he says.

Fear jumps up in my heart, and I try to get to my feet, but Sam gently presses me back down into the bed. The doctor's eyes slide over to him, but she doesn't say anything as she continues to attend to my injuries.

"I have to go," I tell him. "They're waiting for me."

"They're fine," he tells me. "All six women. Eric's team got to them and rescued all of them. They were evacuated to a hospital on the mainland, but we've already gotten an update, and they are all doing well."

"And everybody else?" I ask. "All the other girls at the resort?"

"They've been told they aren't being held anymore and can leave the resort. Unfortunately, for some, this was the only life they have. They've been abandoned here and have no idea where to go or what to do. No family left. No home."

"We'll help them," I say. "That's what comes next. We'll help them figure it out."

Sam leans down and kisses me.

"Yes, we will."

"What about Frederick and Catherine and Constance?" I ask.

"They've been arrested for their roles in the trafficking. There is more than enough evidence against them, especially when the women testify. None of them will talk, but they'll get it out of them. Soon enough, they'll realize they're looking at drug charges, international human trafficking, and murder, and it's in their best interest to help us as much as they can."

The doctor finally finishes and walks away, leaving us alone in the infirmary cubicle. Sam holds my hand and strokes the side of my face.

"Where's Alonso? I want to make sure the investigators know how much he helped. He's guilty as hell, but they need to know he wasn't involved in the prostitution ring."

"He's missing," Sam sighs. "He was here, but the last time I saw him was when we were getting into position. When I looked for him after you came here, I found out he slipped away."

"They'll find him," I say.

"You sure about that?" he asks.

"Yes," I confirm. "I've done my part. What's going on here is just a little part of something much bigger. The FBI can create a special task force to take it from here and uncover the larger trafficking ring. As for the drugs, I'm sure that will come out when they test the women."

"Are you sure you don't want to be more involved in the investigation?"

There's a note to his voice that's hard to read. It's almost hesitant, like he's unsure where my head is. But it's also encouraging. I know this case like no one else does. I'm the one who started it, who first saw that something was wrong. It would seem right that I would be the one to head up the further investigation into the rest of the drugs and the human trafficking.

At least, there was a time when it would have seemed right. Not now.

"I'm sure," I tell him, and I am almost surprised to realize I really mean it. "If they need me, they know where to find me. But I'm ready to go home. I need a vacation from my vacation.

"What's next for you?" he asks.

"Rest. Recover. Then get back to work."

"Have you decided to move back?" Sam asked.

The sadness in his eyes makes my heart ache, and I reach up to touch his face. I cup the side of his face as I shake my head.

"No. Sherwood is my home. That's not going to change. But I don't want to just sit around anymore. I don't want to just do video chats and online research when they feel like they can use me. I'm ready to tell Creagan I'm ready to get active again."

"What about going into private investigation with Dean?"

I let out a sigh and nod, acknowledging all the conversations I had with him about the possibility and whether it was the right decision for me. Sam was my sounding board, listening to me as I tried to process through everything. I didn't always need him to tell me what he thought, and he knew that. It wasn't about getting his opinion or getting his input. He knew that there were times when I just needed to be able to talk things through out loud and hear myself say them. But when I did need to know what he thought, he was there to give me that as well.

"Going into private investigation really sounded like a good thing. It would definitely give me a quieter personal life. I could stay out of the more intense investigations and give my time to more focused issues that aren't getting attention. And that could still happen. I can still help him with his cases and do my own when I'm not on active investigations with the Bureau. But, at least for now, it's not all I want."

"What made you change your mind?" he asks.

"I didn't change my mind. Not really, anyway. I questioned if my days with the Bureau were finished because I thought I'd finished everything I intended to when I started. I thought since now that I know what happened to my mother and my father is back, I don't need the Bureau. Then I came here. Seeing Rosa's murder being ignored reminded me why I became an agent to begin with. There is too much darkness out there, too many people getting away with brutalizing others and destroying lives for me to turn my back now. I'm not done yet."

EPILOGUE
DRAGON

He stands on the roof and looks down over his resort. From his vantage point, he can see nearly to the edges of the island, but all he cares about is what was just below him. That sheriff has his arm tightly around Emma's waist as he helps her out of the infirmary and into the waiting car. It will bring her to the lobby, where Joshua waits to bring them to the airport.

Everything will change now. But not the way people think. The resort will not close. The island will not become once again deserted and empty. He will thrive.

He was not to blame for any of this. And he could prove that.

Not with his name. Not with his face. He can't do that. It would be too dangerous.

Then he could never have her.

Emma is his only focus, the only thing beyond his reach, the only thing he cannot buy.

Others would stand in his place and offer themselves up for scrutiny. They would claim the island, the resort, the darkness now hanging over it. And with his guidance, they would slide out of that darkness just the way he would have. Catherine, Constance, and Frederick took advantage of what he created. They were greedy and selfish and did something he could never forgive.

But not Alonso. Alonso could still be trusted.

And one day, Emma would be his. Her betrayal would be soothed. All the pain she created atoned for. It wasn't her fault. He knows that. She still wants him. She always has.

This should have worked. She shouldn't be leaving in the back of that car with the sheriff comforting her. But he can be patient.

He has been for this long.

THE END

To my amazing readers,

I first just want to say THANK YOU!
I am able to keep writing these novels, because of you!
Writing this novel and the past Emma Griffin series brought me a ton of joy.
I truly hope that I have brought you the same amount of thrill and joy into your life while reading my novels.
I know the world is a bit mad at this moment. I hope that I was also able to take your mind out of the chaos and give you a moment of peace.

There is something that I would greatly appreciate from you at this moment.
I would massively appreciate if you could take a moment of your day to write a review for this novel.
Your reviews give me the motivation to keep this series going, and it helps me massively as an indie author.
Your reviews alone have helped me tremendously when I was first starting out.

The review doesn't have to be long, but however short or long you want.
Just a few seconds of your time is all that is needed.
When you leave me a review, know that I am eternally grateful to YOU.

Thank you for taking the time to read my novel!
My promise to you has always been to do my best to bring you thrilling adventures.
I hope I have fulfilled that. I look forward to you reading my next novel!

Yours,
A.J. Rivers

P.S. If, for some reason, you didn't like this book or found typos or other errors, please let me know personally. I do my best to read and respond to every email at aj@riversthrillers.com

ALSO BY A.J. RIVERS

Emma Griffin FBI Mysteries

Season One

Book One - The Girl in Cabin 13*

Book Two - The Girl Who Vanished

Book Three - The Girl in the Manor

Book Four - The Girl Next Door

Book Five - The Girl and the Deadly Express

Book Six - The Girl and the Hunt

Book Seven - The Girl and the Deadly End

Season Two

Book Eight - The Girl in Dangerous Waters

Other Standalone Novels

Gone Woman